MAIGRET
and the
RELUCTANT
WITNESSES

Georges Simenon

MAIGRET and the RELUCTANT WITNESSES

Translated from the French by Daphne Woodward

A Harvest/HBJ Book
A Helen and Kurt Wolff Book
Harcourt Brace Jovanovich, Publishers
San Diego   New York   London

HBJ

Copyright © 1959 by Georges Simenon
English translation copyright © 1959 by Daphne Woodward

All rights reserved. No part of this publication may be
reproduced or transmitted in any form or by any means,
electronic or mechanical, including photocopy, recording,
or any information storage and retrieval system, without
permission in writing from the publisher.

Requests for permission to make copies of any part of the work
should be mailed to: Copyrights and Permissions Department,
Harcourt Brace Jovanovich, Publishers, Orlando, Florida 32887.

Library of Congress Cataloging-in-Publication Data
Simenon, Georges, 1903–1989.
[Maigret et les témoins récalcitrants. English]
Maigret and the reluctant witnesses/Georges Simenon; translated
from the French by Daphne Woodward.
p.   cm.
Translation of: Maigret et les témoins récalcitrants.
"A Helen and Kurt Wolff book."
ISBN 0-15-655159-4 (pbk.)
I. Title.
PQ2637.I53M258913   1989
843'.912—dc20   89-38060

Printed in the United States of America
First Harvest/HBJ edition 1989

A B C D E F G H I J

MAIGRET
and the
RELUCTANT
WITNESSES

1

'Y o u haven't forgotten your umbrella?'

'No.'

In a moment the door would close behind Maigret; he had already turned towards the stairs.

'You'd better wear your muffler.'

Madame Maigret bustled away to fetch it, with no inkling that those simple words would stick in her husband's mind for quite a time, with depressing effect.

It was only November—November 3rd—and the weather wasn't particularly cold. But rain was falling from a sky of low, unbroken grey, one of those steady showers that seem wetter and somehow more perfidious, especially first thing in the morning, than ordinary rain.

A while ago, getting out of bed, he had winced because his neck hurt when he turned his head. You couldn't call it a proper stiff neck, but he couldn't move it quite as usual, something felt wrong.

The evening before, after the cinema, they had walked for a good distance along the Boulevards, and it had been raining already.

All this was of no importance. And yet, because of the muffler, perhaps also because it was a thick muffler that his wife had knitted for him, he felt old.

Going downstairs, where there were damp footmarks on the steps, and then outside, walking under his umbrella, he remembered what she had said to him last evening. In two years' time he'd be retiring.

He had shared her pleasure at the idea. For a long time they had chatted lazily about the part of the country where they were going to live, near Meung-sur-Loire, a district they were both fond of.

A bare-headed little boy ran into him and didn't apologize. A young married couple went past, arm-in-arm, sharing an umbrella; they doubtless worked in offices near each other.

It had been an emptier Sunday than usual, possibly because this year it happened to be All Souls' Day. He would have sworn that he could still smell the chrysanthemums this morning. From their window they had watched the family groups setting off for the cemeteries; but neither of them had any relations buried in Paris.

He waited for his bus at the corner of the Boulevard Voltaire, and felt glummer than ever when he saw the large vehicle drive up; it was

2

one of the new kind without a platform, so that he was not only obliged to sit down, but had to knock out his pipe as well.

We all have days like that, don't we?

He longed for the next two years to be over; then he wouldn't have to wind a muffler round his neck and set out across Paris on beastly wet mornings like this, with the place looking the same black and white as in an old silent film.

The bus was full of young people; some recognized him, others took no notice.

On the quays the rain slanted down more sharply and felt colder. He hurried into the arched, draughty entrance of Police Headquarters, strode towards the stairs; and then, all of a sudden, recognizing the characteristic smell of the building, the greenish glimmer of the lamps, which were still alight, he felt sad to think that in such a short time he would stop coming here each morning.

Old Joseph, who for some mysterious reason had escaped the retired-list, greeted him with a conspiratorial air and murmured:

'Inspector Lapointe is waiting for you, Chief-Inspector.'

As usual on Mondays, there were a lot of people in the waiting-room and in the long corridor. Some new faces; two or three young women who were hardly the type one would expect to see there, but mostly old acquaintances who turned up every now and then at one door or another.

He went into his office, hung his overcoat in

the cupboard together with his hat and that muffler, hesitated whether to open the umbrella and leave it out to dry, according to Madame Maigret's instructions, finally stood it in a corner of the cupboard.

It was barely half past eight. There were letters waiting on his blotter. He went across and opened the door into the inspectors' office, greeted Lucas, Torrence and two or three others with a gesture of the hand.

'Somebody tell Lapointe I'm here.'

That would touch off a rumour that the Chief was in a bad mood today, which was not true. Sometimes, looking back on days when one has been grumpy, glum, touchy, one sees them in memory as among the happiest.

'Good morning, Chief.'

Lapointe was pale, his eyes a little bloodshot from lack of sleep, but sparkling with satisfaction. He was quivering with impatience.

'Done it! I've got him!'

'Where is he?'

'In the little room at the end of the corridor; Torrence has gone to keep an eye on him.'

'What time?'

'Four o'clock this morning.'

'Has he talked?'

'I had coffee sent up, and then, about six o'clock, breakfast for both of us, and we chatted like old friends.'

'Go and fetch him.'

This was nice work. Grégoire Brau, known as Patience, also as the Canon, had been at his

4

game for years without ever being caught in the act.

Only once, twelve years ago, he had been nabbed because he had overslept, but when he came out of prison he had gone right back to his old ways.

He came into the office now, preceded by Lapointe looking as proud as though he'd caught the biggest trout or pike of the year, and stood, sheepishly, in front of Maigret, who was deep in his papers.

'Sit down.'

The chief-inspector added, as he finished scanning a letter:

'Have you got any cigarettes?'

'Yes, Monsieur Maigret.'

'You can smoke.'

Brau was a fat fellow of forty-three, who must have been plump and flabby even in his schooldays. He had a fresh complexion, a pink face that reddened easily, a blunt nose, a double chin, a guileless mouth.

'So they got you after all?'

'They got me.'

It was Maigret who had arrested him the first time, and they had often met again since then, greeting each other without ill-feeling.

'You've been at it again!' continued the chief-inspector, alluding to the burglary of a flat.

Instead of denying the statement, the Canon smiled modestly. There was no proof. But though he never left a single finger-print his jobs were signed, as it were.

5

He worked alone, planning each job with incredible patience. He was the very image of a quiet man, with no vices, no passions, no nerves.

He spent most of his time sitting in a corner of some bar, café or restaurant, apparently deep in a newspaper, or dozing; but his keen ears lost nothing of what was being said around him.

Moreover he was a great reader of weekly magazines; he studied their society and gossip columns with care and had an unparalleled knowledge of the comings and goings of celebrities.

Sooner or later Police Headquarters would be rung up by some famous person, sometimes an actor or film star, who had just got back from Hollywood, London, Rome or Cannes to find that their flat had been broken into.

Without needing to hear the whole story, Maigret would ask:

'What about the refrigerator?'

'Empty!'

All the liqueurs would have vanished from the cellar too. One could be sure, too, that the bed would have been slept in, and the pyjamas, dressing-gown and slippers of the owner would have been used.

That was the Canon's signature, an obsession that had come over him right at the start, when he was only twenty-two, perhaps because in those days he was really hungry and longed for a comfortable bed. When he was sure that a flat was empty for several weeks, that no servants were left there, that the concierge had not been told to go up and air it, he would move in, without the aid of a jemmy, for no lock could keep its secrets from him.

Once inside, instead of hastily making off with any valuables such as jewellery, pictures, ornaments, he would settle down for a time, usually until the supply of provisions was exhausted.

As many as thirty empty tins had been found after one of his visits; and a number of bottles too, of course. He read. He slept. He made use of the bathroom with a kind of voluptuous satisfaction, unsuspected by the other occupants of the house.

Then he would go home and resume his regular habits, going out only in the evenings, for a game of *belote*, to a rather ill-famed bar in the Avenue des Ternes, where, because he worked alone and never talked about his exploits, he was regarded with a mixture of respect and distrust.

'Did she write to you, or ring up?'

He put this question in a kind of melancholy that resembled the feeling with which Maigret had left home a while earlier.

'What are you talking about?'

'You know very well, Monsieur Maigret. Otherwise you wouldn't have picked me up. Your inspector'—he looked at Lapointe-'was in the house, on the stairs, before I got there, and I suppose he'd left one of his pals in the street outside? Correct?'

'Correct.'

Lapointe had spent not one night, but two,

on the stairs of the house at Passy where a certain Monsieur Ailevard owned a flat. That gentleman had gone to London for a fortnight. The newspapers had announced his trip, for it was connected with a film and with a very well-known star.

The Canon didn't always rush into a house the moment people had left it. He took his time and his precautions.

'Can't think how I missed seeing your inspector. Well, that'll teach me . . . Did she ring you up?'

Maigret shook his head.

'She wrote to you?'

He nodded.

'I suppose you couldn't show me the letter? She must have disguised her writing, of course?'

Not even that. No point in telling him, though.

'I rather thought, without letting myself believe it, that this would happen one day. She's a bitch, if you'll excuse my language, and yet I can't hold it against her . . . After all, I've had two pretty good years, when you come to think of it.'

He had gone on for years without any woman in his life, and because of his appearance some people used to tease him for this, declaring that there were good reasons for his virtuous behaviour.

Suddenly, at the age of forty-one, he had set up house with a certain Germaine, twenty years his junior, who had had her pitch on the Avenue de Wagram for a short time past.

'Did you marry her in the registry office?'

'And in church. She's from Brittany. I suppose she's already moved in on Henri?'

He was referring to a young pimp known as Henri-My-Eye.

'No, he's moved into your place.'

The Canon displayed no indignation, did not rail against fate, blamed only himself.

'What'll I get?'

'From two to five years. Did Inspector Lapointe take down your statement?'

'He made notes of what I told him.'

The telephone rang.

'Hello? Chief-Inspector Maigret here.'

He listened, frowned.

'The name again, please.'

He pulled a pad towards him, scribbled: 'Lachaume.'

'Quai de la Gare? . . . At Ivry? . . . Very well. . . . Is there a doctor there? . . . Fellow's definitely dead, is he? . . .'

The Canon's importance had instantly dwindled, as he himself seemed to realize. He got up without being told.

'I suppose you've other things to see to . . .'

Maigret turned to Lapointe.

'Take him to the *Dépôt*, then go and get some sleep.'

He opened the cupboard to take out his hat and coat, then, on second thoughts, held out his hand to the fat man with pink cheeks.

'It isn't our fault, old man.'

'I know.'

He didn't put on the muffler. Going to the inspectors' room he chose Janvier, who had only just arrived and was not yet at work.

'You're coming with me.'

'Yes, Chief.'

'Lucas, you ring up the Public Prosecutor's office. A man has been killed by a bullet in the heart, on the Quai de la Gare at Ivry. Name of Lachaume . . . Lachaume's Biscuits. . . .'

This called up memories that took him right back to his country childhood. In those days, in every dimly lit village grocery, where dried vegetables were offered for sale alongside clogs and sewing-cotton, you were sure to find cellophane-wrapped packets labelled 'Biscuiterie Lachaume'.

Lachaume's made *petits-beurre* and wafer-biscuits, both of which had the same rather cardboardy taste.

He had not heard of them since those days. Neither had he seen any more of those calendars showing a little boy with exaggeratedly rosy cheeks and an inane grin, eating a Lachaume wafer, and it was even rare nowadays to see the name in faded letters on a wall in some isolated village.

'Tell the Identity people too, of course.'

'Yes, Chief.'

Lucas was reaching for the telephone already. Maigret and Janvier went downstairs.

'Are we taking the car?'

Maigret's depression had evaporated in the everyday atmosphere of Police Headquarters.

Caught up in the routine, he had forgotten to be introspective or to put questions to himself.

Sundays have a pernicious influence. Sitting in the car and lighting a pipe that tasted delicious again, he asked:

'D'you know Lachaume's Biscuits?'

'No, Chief.'

'You're too young, of course.'

Besides, perhaps they had never been on sale in Paris? A whole lot of things are manufactured just for country districts. Then there are the makes that go out of fashion, but still have a limited following. He could remember some *apéritifs* that were celebrated in his young days, but you never came across them now except in some lost inn, far from any main road.

After crossing the bridge they could not follow the river, because of the one-way system along the quays, and Janvier had to go a long way round before getting back to the Seine, opposite Charenton. On the other side they could see the Halle aux Vins, and to the left a train was going over an iron bridge across the river.

In the old days there had been nothing here except small detached houses and brick and timber yards; now there were blocks of flats, six or seven storeys high, with shops and *bistrots* on the ground floor; but every so often came a gap, a patch of waste ground, some studios, or two or three low houses.

'What number?'

Maigret told him, and they pulled up in front of what must once have been a handsome house, a three-storey affair in brick and stone, with behind it a tall chimney, like a factory chimney. There was a car at the door. A policeman was walking to and fro along the pavement. It was difficult to tell whether this was still Paris or already Ivry, and the turning they had just passed was probably the dividing street.

'Good morning, Chief-Inspector. The door isn't locked. They're waiting for you upstairs.'

The house had a carriage entrance, with a gate painted green and a smaller door let in on one side. Going in, the two men found themselves in an arched passage, not unlike that of the Quai des Orfèvres, except that the far end was closed by a door with frosted glass panes. One of the panes was missing and the gap had been filled with a piece of cardboard.

It was cold and damp. A door opened off on either side of the passage, and Maigret, wondering which to choose, opened the one on the right; evidently the right choice, for it revealed a kind of hall and the foot of a wide staircase.

The walls, once white, had taken on a yellow tinge with browner patches here and there, and the cracking plaster had fallen off in places. The three lowest steps were of marble; the others were wooden, looked as though they had not been swept for a long time, and creaked when trodden on.

It was rather like one of those municipal offices where you always feel, on entering, that you have come to the wrong place. Each man felt that if he spoke his voice might echo back at him.

Footsteps were heard on the first floor and a man leant over the banisters, a youngish, tired-looking man, who introduced himself as soon as Maigret reached the top of the stairs.

'My name's Legrand, I'm the secretary of the Ivry Police Station. . . . The superintendent is waiting for you. . . .'

Another hall upstairs, with a marble floor, an uncurtained window looking out at the Seine and the falling rain.

It was an enormous house, with doors on all sides, corridors like some government building, and everywhere the same drab aspect and the same smell of long-settled dust.

At the end of a narrower passage, on the left, the secretary knocked at a door and opened it, revealing a bedroom so dark that the local superintendent had kept the light on.

This room looked into the courtyard, and through the dusty muslin curtains could be seen the chimney that Maigret had already noticed from outside.

He was vaguely acquainted with the Ivry superintendent, who was of a younger generation and shook his hand with exaggerated respect.

'I came as soon as I had the telephone call. . . .'

'Has the doctor left?'

'He had an urgent case. I didn't think I need keep him, because in any case the official pathologist will be here soon. . . .'

The body was lying on the bed, and except for the superintendent there was no one in the room.

'What about the family?'

'I told them to go to their own rooms or to the drawing-room. I thought you'd rather . . .'

Maigret took his watch out of his pocket. It was a quarter to ten.

'When did you hear about it?'

'An hour or so ago. I'd just got to the office. Someone rang up my secretary to ask me to come round here.'

'Did he say who he was?'

'Yes. The brother, Armand Lachaume.'

'D'you know him?'

'Only by name. He must have come to the station sometimes, to have a signature witnessed for some formality or other. They're not people one takes much notice of. . . .'

Maigret was struck by the phrase. *Not people one takes much notice of.* He could understand it, for like Lachaume's Biscuits, the house seemed to be at one remove from time, from present-day life.

It was years since Maigret had seen such a bedroom, which must have remained for a century without the slightest change. There was even a washstand with drawers, topped with a slab of grey marble on which stood a flowered china jug and basin, and dishes of the same china to hold soap and combs.

The furniture and other objects were not in themselves particularly ugly. Some of them would perhaps have fetched good prices at an auction, or in an antique shop, but there was something dreary and oppressive about the way they were arranged.

It seemed as though suddenly, long ago, life in this place had stopped, not the life of the man on the bed, but the life of the house, the life surrounding it, and even the factory chimney, seen through the curtains, looked absurd and old-fashioned, with its 'L' inlaid in black bricks.

'Theft?'

Two or three drawers were open. Ties and linen were scattered on the floor in front of the wardrobe.

'It seems that a pocket-book with a biggish sum in it has disappeared.'

'Who is he?'

Maigret pointed to dead man on the bed. The sheets and blankets were in disorder. The pillow had fallen on the ground. One arm was dangling. There was blood on the pyjama jacket where it had been torn or burnt by the powder.

Just as Maigret had been thinking earlier that morning of the sharply-contrasted black and white of silent films, now, in this room, he was suddenly reminded of those illustrations in the old-time Sunday papers, before photographs began to be reproduced and the week's sensations were depicted in engravings.

'Léonard Lachaume, the eldest son.'

'Married?'

'A widower.'

'When did it happen?'

'In the night. According to Dr. Voisin, death took place at about two in the morning.'

'Who was in the house?'

'Let me see. . . . The old couple, his father and mother, on the floor above, in the left wing. . . . That's two. . . . The little boy. . . .'

'What little boy?'

'The dead man's son. . . . A boy of twelve. . . . At the moment, he's at school. . . .'

'In spite of the tragedy?'

'Apparently no one knew about that at eight o'clock, when he went off to school.'

'So no one heard anything? . . . Who else lives here?'

'The maid. . . . I think her name is Catherine. . . . She sleeps up above, near the old couple and the boy. . . . She looks as old as the house and just as rickety. . . . Then there's Armand, the younger brother. . . .'

'Whose brother?'

'The dead man's. . . . He sleeps on the other side of the corridor, and so does his wife.'

'They were all here last night, and the shot didn't wake one of them?'

'So they say. I only asked them a few questions. It's difficult. You'll see!'

'What's difficult?'

'To know. When I got here, I had no idea what it was about. Armand Lachaume, the one who rang me up, opened the downstairs door the moment my car stopped. He seemed as though he were still half-asleep, and said, without looking at me:

' "My brother has been killed, Superintendent."

'He brought me here and pointed to the bed. I asked him when it had happened and he said he hadn't the remotest idea.

'I insisted:

' "But you were in the house?"

' "I suppose so. I slept in my room." '

The police superintendent seemed to be annoyed with himself.

'I don't know how to explain. Usually, when there's a tragedy like this in a family, you find everyone gathered round the corpse, some in tears, others explaining, a bit too talkative if anything. . . .

'Whereas in this case it took me quite a time to discover that the men weren't alone in the house. . . .'

'Have you seen the others?'

'The wife.'

'You mean the wife of Armand, the one who telephoned you?'

'Yes. At some stage I heard a rustling sound in the corridor. I opened the door and found her outside. She had the same air of weariness as her husband. She didn't seem embarrassed. I asked her who she was, and Armand answered for her:

' "She's my wife. . . ."

'I asked whether she hadn't heard anything in the night and she said no, she always took some tablets—I forget what—so as to sleep. . . .'

'Who found the body? And when?'

'The old servant, at a quarter to nine.'

'Have you seen her?'

'Yes. She must have gone back to her kitchen. I suspect she's a bit deaf. She got worried when the eldest son didn't appear at breakfast, which they all have together in the dining-room. In the end she came and knocked on his door. Then she went in, and it was she who told the others.'

'What about the old people?'

'They don't say a word. The wife is half-paralysed and stares straight ahead of her as though she hadn't got all her wits. Her husband seems so distressed that he can hardly follow what one says to him.'

Once more the superintendent added:

'You'll see!'

Maigret turned to Janvier.

'Will you go and have a look round?'

Janvier departed and the chief-inspector at last went over to the body, which was lying on its left side, facing the window. Someone had already closed the man's eyes. His mouth was half-open, beneath a drooping brown moustache with some grey hairs in it. His thin hair clung to his temples and forehead.

It was difficult to gauge the expression on his face. He did not seem to have felt pain, and looked more astonished than anything else. But perhaps that came from the open mouth, and he hadn't looked like that till he was dead?

Maigret heard steps in the upstairs hall, then along the corridor. Opening the door, he encountered one of the public prosecutor's deputies, whom he had known for a long time and who shook his hand silently, looking across at the bed. He knew the clerk too, and nodded to him, but he had never set eyes on the tall young man who came in behind them, hatless and coatless.

'This is Monsieur Angelot, the examining magistrate. . . .'

The young man, thus named, extended a firm, well-manicured hand, the hand of a tennis-player, and Maigret reflected once again that a new generation was already taking over.

However, old Dr. Paul came in shortly afterwards, out of breath, but alert, with a well-fed look about his eyes and mouth.

'Where's the stiff?'

Maigret noticed that the grey-blue eyes of the examining magistrate remained cold and that he frowned slightly, doubtless in disapproval.

'Have the photographers finished?' went on Dr. Paul.

'They haven't arrived yet. I think I can hear them now.'

That meant waiting till the photographers were through, and then the Judicial Identity experts invaded the room and set to work.

In a corner, the public prosecutor's deputy asked Maigret:

'A family quarrel?'

'Apparently there's been theft.'

'No one heard anything?'

'They say not.'

'How many people in the house?'

'Wait till I count. . . . The old couple and the servant, that's three. . . . The little boy. . . .'

'What little boy?'

'The dead man's son. . . . That's four. . . . Then the brother and his wife. . . . Six! Six people beside the fellow who got killed, and none of them heard a thing. . . .'

The public prosecutor's deputy went over to the doorway and ran his hand over the wall-paper.

'The walls are thick, but all the same! . . . No weapon been found?'

'I don't know. . . . The Ivry police superintendent said nothing about that. I'm waiting till the formalities are over, before beginning my investigation. . . .'

The photographers were looking for electric points where they could plug in their lamps, and finding none, they had to take the bulb out of the centre light. They strode about, grumbling, getting in one another's way, calling out hasty instructions, while the examining magistrate, who looked like an athletic student, stood waiting, grey-suited and motionless, without a word.

'Do you think I could go now?' asked the local superintendent.

'There must be a mob in my waiting-room. I could send you two or three men in case the rubber-neckers start collecting outside the house a bit later on. . . .'

'That would be very kind. Thank you.'

'Would you like to have one of my inspectors as well, one who knows the neighbourhood?'

'I expect I shall need one later. I'll ring you up. Thank you again.'

As he went out, the superintendent said once again:

'You'll see!'

The public prosecutor's deputy asked in an undertone:

'See what?'

'The family. . . . The whole set-up. . . . There was no one in the room when the police superintendent arrived. . . . They're all in their own rooms, or in the dining-room. . . . Nobody stirs. . . . There isn't a sound. . . .'

The deputy glanced at the furniture, the damp-marked wallpaper, the mirror above the fireplace, where generations of flies had left traces of their passage.

'It doesn't surprise me. . . .'

The photographers were the first to leave, which cleared the room a bit. Dr. Paul was able to make a preliminary examination, while the Identity experts looked for finger-prints and went through drawers and cupboards.

'What time, Doctor?'

'I shall be able to say more definitely after the post-mortem, but he's been dead a good six hours, if not more.'

'Killed instantaneously?'

'The shot was fired at very close range. . . . The external wound is as big as a saucer, the flesh scorched. . . .'

21

'What about the bullet?'

'I shall find it inside him presently, for it didn't go right through, which suggests that it was of small calibre.'

His hands were covered with blood. He went across to the wash-stand, but the jug was empty.

'There must be a tap somewhere. . . .'

One of the others opened the door for him. Armand Lachaume, the younger brother, was in the corridor, and it was he who, without a word, led him to an old-fashioned bathroom where stood an antique, claw-footed bath-tub, whose tap must have been dribbling for years past, for it had left rusty streaks on the enamel.

'I'll leave you to it, Maigret,' sighed the public prosecutor's deputy, turning towards the examining magistrate. 'I'm going back to the *Palais de Justice*.'

Whereupon the magistrate murmured:

'I hope you don't mind if I don't come with you. I'm staying here.'

Maigret started, and almost blushed to see that the young judge had noticed it. The latter went on at once:

'I hope you have no objection, Chief-Inspector. I'm only a beginner, you know, and this will be valuable experience for me.'

Wasn't there the faintest trace of irony in his voice? He was polite, too polite even. And completely cold beneath his surface friendliness.

He was one of the new school, the school that regards an investigation as the affair of the examining magistrate from start to finish, with the role of the police reduced to obeying his instructions.

Janvier, who appeared in the doorway at that moment and had heard what was said, exchanged a highly expressive glance with Maigret.

2

MAIGRET could not hide his annoyance and almost lost his temper altogether at the thought that the examining magistrate was not only noticing it, but must inevitably be putting it down to his own presence, which in fact was only part of the reason. For hadn't that muffler business, even as he left the Boulevard Richard-Lenoir, started a procession of gloomy reflections?

This fellow Angelot, so fresh and brisk, had only just left college. Either he was an exceptional chap, one of the few in each generation, whom you can count on your fingers, or else he was being backed by people in high places; otherwise, instead of getting a job in Paris, he'd have been sent to kick his heels for years in some sub-prefecture magistrate's court.

Just now, when the deputy had introduced them, the examining magistrate had simply shaken Maigret's hand with an energy that might be taken for warmth, but hadn't said any of the things people usually said to the chief-inspector. Naturally he couldn't say, as the older men did:

'Nice to run into you again.'

But there were some who always murmured:

'So glad to be working with you.'

It was hard to believe that Angelot had never heard of him. Yet he had shown neither satisfaction nor curiosity.

Was it a deliberate pose, intended to show Maigret that he wasn't impressed by his reputation? Or simply lack of curiosity, the genuine indifference of the young generation?

Catching certain glances, the chief-inspector wondered whether it might be more in the nature of shyness, a kind of modesty.

That embarrassed him even more than smartness would have done. Feeling himself under observation he struggled for composure.

He said to Lapointe in an undertone:

'You go through the routine stuff. . . .'

They both knew what that meant.

Then he turned to Armand Lachaume, who was unshaven and wearing no tie.

'I suppose there's some room where we could talk more comfortably?' And, noticing the raw cold, he added:

'One that's heated, for choice.'

He had just touched the radiator, an old-fashioned type, and discovered that the central heating was not working.

Lachaume did not go out of his way to be

polite either. He seemed to think for a moment, then, his shoulders slumped in resignation, he said:

'This way. . . .'

There was something ambiguous, not only in the atmosphere of the house, but in the attitude of its occupants. As the Ivry superintendent had remarked, one expected weeping, confused hurrying to and fro, people talking all at once; whereas here were only stealthy footsteps, doors opening slightly, faces peering through the crack.

For instance, going along the dimly lit corridor, Maigret glimpsed, through the narrow chink of a doorway, an eye, dark hair, a silhouette which seemed to be that of a woman.

They reached the upstairs hall, and Armand Lachaume opened a door in the left wing, to reveal a strange drawing-room where two old people were sitting in front of an iron stove.

The son said nothing, made no introductions. The father was a man of at least seventy-five, perhaps eighty. Unlike Armand, he was freshly shaved and had on a clean shirt, a black tie.

He stood up, as placid and dignified as though this were a directors' meeting, bowed slightly, then stepped forward to bend over his wife, who seemed to be the same age as himself; one side of her face was motionless, with a staring eye like a glass eye.

He helped her out of her arm-chair, and both of them, without a word, vanished through another door.

This was the room where the family usually

assembled; that was evident from the arrangement of the furniture and from the oddments lying about. Maigret sat down on a chair and turned to Angelot, the examining magistrate.

'Do you wish to ask any questions?'

'I would rather leave it to you.'

The magistrate stood leaning against the side of the door.

'Would you mind sitting down, Monsieur Lachaume?' pursued Maigret.

It was like groping his way through cotton-wool. There was nothing to get hold of, nothing seemed real except the rain still falling outside.

'Please tell me what you know.'

'I know nothing.'

Even the man's voice was expressionless, impersonal, and he was avoiding Maigret's eye.

'The dead man is your elder brother, is he not?'

'My brother Léonard, as I already told your colleague.'

'Is the biscuit factory still going?'

'Certainly.'

'Was it he who ran it?'

'Our father is still chairman of the board of directors.'

'But who was the actual manager?'

'My brother.'

'And you?'

'I look after stocks and distribution.'

'Is it long since your brother lost his wife?'

'Eight years.'

'Are you acquainted with his private life?'

'He has always lived here, with us.'

'All the same, outside this house he presumably had a life of his own, men and women friends, connexions of various kinds?'

'I don't know.'

'You told the police superintendent that a wallet had disappeared.'

He nodded.

'About how much money might be in the wallet?'

'I can't say.'

'A large sum?'

'I don't know.'

'Was your brother in the habit, for instance, of keeping several hundred thousand francs in his room?'

'I don't think so.'

'Was it he who handled the firm's money?'

'He and the book-keeper.'

'Where is the book-keeper?'

'I presume he is downstairs.'

'And where was the money put when it came in?'

'In the bank.'

'Every day?'

'Money doesn't come in every day.'

Maigret was forcing himself to remain calm and courteous, beneath the dispassionate gaze of the young magistrate.

'But surely there was some money somewhere . . .'

'In the safe.'

'Where is the safe?'

'On the ground floor, in my brother's office.'

'Was it tampered with during the night?'

'No.'

'You have made sure of that?'

'Yes.'

'You think your brother's murderer came from outside, with theft as his intention?'

'Yes.'

'Someone he didn't know from Adam?'

'I suppose so.'

'How many people work in the factory?'

'At present, about twenty. At one time we employed over a hundred men and women.'

'You know them all?'

'Yes.'

'You don't suspect one of them?'

'No.'

'You heard nothing last night, although your room is only a few yards away from your brother Léonard's?'

'I heard nothing.'

'You are a heavy sleeper?'

'Perhaps.'

'You sleep heavily enough not to be disturbed by a shot fired less than ten paces away?'

'I don't know.'

Just then there was a rumbling sound, and the house, despite its thick walls, seemed to shake a little. Maigret's eye caught that of the examining magistrate.

'Is that a train?'

'Yes. The line runs close by here.'

'Do many trains go past at night?'

'I've never counted them. About forty, most of them long goods trains.'

There was a knock on the door. It was Janvier, who signed to Maigret that he had something to tell him.

'Come in. Tell us.'

'There's a ladder in the courtyard, lying on the ground a few yards from the wall. I found the marks of the uprights on the window-sill.'

'Which window?'

'A window of the landing, next to this room. It looks into the courtyard. The ladder must have been leant up there recently, and a pane of the window has been broken, after having been coated with soap.'

'You knew this, Monsieur Lachaume?'

'I had noted the fact.'

'Why did you say nothing to me about it?'

'I have had no opportunity of doing so.'

'Where was this ladder, in the usual way?'

'Against the warehouse, on the left of the courtyard.'

'Was it there yesterday evening?'

'Normally it should be there.'

'Excuse me for a moment.'

Maigret left the room, partly to see for himself and partly to let off steam, and he seized the chance to fill a pipe. The upstairs hall was lit by two windows, one overlooking the quay, the other, opposite it, over the courtyard. This latter had a broken pane, and some fragments of glass lay on the floor.

Opening the window, he saw that the grey

stone bore two lighter marks, as far apart as the uprights of a ladder.

As Janvier had told him, a ladder was lying on the flagstones of the courtyard. Faint smoke was rising from the tall chimney. In a building on the left, women were bending over a long table.

He was just going back to the others, when he heard a sound and saw a woman in a blue dressing-gown, who had just opened her door.

'Might I ask you, Madame, to come to the drawing-room for a moment?'

She seemed to hesitate, then tied the belt of her dressing-gown and at last came forward.

She was young. She had not yet made up her face and it was a little shiny.

'Please come in.' And to Armand Lachaume:

'I take it this is your wife?'

'Yes.'

Husband and wife did not look at each other.

'Please sit down, Madame.'

'Thank you.'

'You, too, heard nothing in the night?'

'I always take a sleeping-tablet before going to bed.'

'When did you hear that your brother-in-law was dead?'

She stared into space for a moment, as though pondering this.

'I didn't look at the time.'

'Where were you?'

'In my room.'

'That is your husband's room as well?'

Again she hesitated.

'No.'

'But your room is in the corridor, nearly opposite your brother-in-law's room?'

'Yes. There are two rooms on the right of the corridor, my husband's and mine.'

'How long have you had separate rooms?'

Armand Lachaume coughed, turned towards the examining magistrate, who was still standing up, and said in an ill-assured voice, the voice of a timid man who feels obliged to make an effort.

'I wonder whether the chief-inspector is entitled to ask us these questions concerning our private lives. My brother was killed last night by a burglar, and so far it is only our movements that seem to be the subject of inquiry.'

The ghost of a smile twitched Angelot's lips.

'I imagine that when Chief-Inspector Maigret puts these questions to you he is regarding you as witnesses.'

'I don't want my wife to be pestered, and I'd like her to be left outside all this.'

It was the anger of a shy man, of one who seldom expressed his feelings, and it had brought a flush to his cheeks.

Maigret went on again gently:

'Who had been regarded as the head of the family until now, Monsieur Lachaume?'

'Which family?'

'Let us say, of the group of people living in this house.'

'That is our business. Don't answer him, Paulette.'

Maigret noticed that he spoke to his wife with the formal *vous*, but that is customary in a certain class, is often a kind of snobbish affectation.

'If this kind of thing goes on, you will be annoying my father and mother presently. Then the employees, the staff . . .'

'That is my intention.'

'I do not know your precise rights . . .'

The magistrate volunteered:

'I can tell you what they are.'

'No. I prefer our lawyer to be present. I suppose I am allowed to send for him?'

The examining magistrate hesitated before replying:

'There is nothing in the regulations to prevent the presence of your lawyer. But I would anyway like to point out once again that you and the members of your family are being questioned as witnesses, and that it is not usual, in such circumstances, to call upon . . .'

'We shall say nothing further until he is here.'

'Just as you like.'

'I will go and telephone him.'

'Where is the telephone?'

'In the dining-room.'

This was the room next door, and they had a glimpse of the two old people who had settled in front of the fireplace where two meagre logs were burning. Thinking this was a fresh invasion, they made as if to get up in order to take refuge somewhere else, but Armand Lachaume closed the door behind him.

'Your husband seems to have been considerably shaken, Madame.'

She looked stonily at the chief-inspector.

'It's natural, don't you think?'

'Were they twins, he and his brother?'

'There is seven years' difference between them.'

Yet their features were the same, even to the identical thin, drooping moustaches. A murmur of voices came from the next room. The magistrate showed no sign of impatience, no desire to sit down.

'You have no suspicion, no idea of your own, about . . .'

'My husband told you we would not answer questions except in the presence of our lawyer.'

'Who is he?'

'Ask my husband.'

'Are there any other brothers or sisters?'

She looked at him in silence. And yet she seemed to be of a different race from the rest of the family. One could feel that in other circumstances she would be pretty, desirable, and she had a muted vitality which she was obliged to hold in check.

She was an unexpected figure in this house where everything was so far removed from time and real life.

Armand Lachaume reappeared. There was another glimpse of the two old people, sitting in front of the fireplace like waxen images.

'He will be here in a few minutes.'

34

He gave a start, as the footsteps of several men were heard on the stairs. Maigret reassured him.

'They've come for the body,' he explained. 'I'm sorry, but as the examining magistrate will tell you, this is a regulation: the body must be taken to the medico-legal institute for a post-mortem to be performed.'

The curious thing was that there seemed to be no grief here, only a strange dejection, a kind of uneasy stupor.

Many a time in his career Maigret had been in much the same position, forced to intrude into the life of a family in which a crime had just been committed.

Never had he received such an impression of unreality.

And into the bargain, an examining magistrate, belonging to a younger generation, had to complicate things by dogging his heels.

'I'll have a word with those fellows,' he muttered. 'I must give some instructions . . .'

They needed neither instruction nor advice. The men with the stretcher knew their job. Maigret simply watched them at it, lifted the sheet that covered the dead man's face for a moment, to have a final brief glance at him.

Then, looking round the room, he saw a door at one side, opened it, and found himself in a dusty, untidy room which must have been Léonard Lachaume's private office.

Janvier was there, bending over a piece of furniture, and gave a start:

'Oh! it's you, Chief . . .'

He was opening the drawers of an old desk, one by one.

'Have you found anything?'

'No. I don't like this ladder business.'

Neither did Maigret. He had not yet had a chance to prowl round the house, or outside it, but all the same that ladder struck him as somehow incongruous.

'You see,' went on Janvier, 'there's a glass-panelled door just below the window with the broken pane. It opens into the entry, and anyone can come up here from there with nothing to stop them. Coming in that way it wouldn't even have been necessary to break a pane in the door, for there was already that broken one that's filled in with cardboard. So why carry a very heavy ladder across the courtyard and . . .'

'I know.'

'Is *he* going to hang around till the bitter end?'

He, of course, was the examining magistrate.

'I don't know. He may.'

This time both of them jumped, for there was someone standing in the doorway, a little old woman, almost a hunchback, who was glaring at them with dark, indignant eyes.

It was the servant to whom the police superintendent had referred. Her glance travelled from the two men to the open drawers, the scattered papers, and at last she muttered, with a visible effort to keep from reviling them:

'Would Chief-Inspector Maigret come to the drawing-room, please.'

Janvier inquired in a low voice:

'Shall I go on, Chief?'

'At the present stage I really don't know. Do as you like.'

He followed the waiting hunchback, who opened the door for him into the drawing-room, where there was a newcomer. He introduced himself:

'Maître Radel . . .'

Was he going to refer to himself in the third person?

'Pleased to meet you, Maître.'

Another young fellow, though not so young as the magistrate. In this house, this survival from another age, Maigret would have expected some old, dirty, pettifogging lawyer.

Radel could hardly be over thirty-five and he was almost as well turned-out as the examining magistrate.

'Gentlemen, I only know what Monsieur Armand Lachaume thought fit to tell me on the telephone, and I would like first of all to apologize for my client's reactions. Try to put yourselves in his place, and you will perhaps understand him. I have come here as a friend rather than as a lawyer, and in order to clear up any misunderstanding. Armand Lachaume is a sick man. The death of his brother, who was the life and soul of this house, has been a great shock to him, and it is not surprising that, in his ignorance of police methods, he should have been riled by certain questions.'

Maigret sighed in resignation to the inevitable, and relit his pipe which had gone out.

'Since he has asked me to be present at any interrogations you may decide to hold, I will do so, but I must emphasize that my presence is not to be regarded as implying any defensive attitude on the part of the family . . .'

He turned to the examining magistrate, then to the chief-inspector.

'Whom do you wish to question?'

'Madame Lachaume,' said Maigret, indicating the young woman.

'I will only ask you to bear in mind that Madame Lachaume is just as distressed as her husband.'

'I would like,' went on Maigret, 'to question each person separately.'

The husband scowled. Maître Radel spoke to him quietly and persuaded him to leave the room.

'To your knowledge, Madame, had your brother-in-law received any threatening letters recently?'

'Certainly not.'

'He would have told you?'

'I imagine so.'

'Told you, or the rest of the family?'

'He would have told us all.'

'Including his parents?'

'Perhaps not, in view of their age.'

'So he would have told your husband and yourself.'

'That would have been natural, I think.'

'The brothers were on close, confident terms?'

'Very close and very confident.'

'And with you?'

'I don't know what you mean.'

'On what terms were you, exactly, with your brother-in-law?'

'I apologize for interrupting,' put in Maître Radel, 'but expressed in those words, that might seem to be a leading question. I take it, Monsieur Maigret, that it is not your intention to insinuate . . .'

'I am not insinuating anything at all. I am merely asking whether Madame Lachaume and her brother-in-law were on friendly terms.'

'Certainly we were,' she replied.

'On affectionate terms?'

'The same as in any other family, I suppose.'

'When did you see him for the last time?'

'Well . . . this morning . . .'

'You mean that this morning you saw him dead in his room?'

She nodded.

'When did you last see him alive?'

'Last night.'

'At what time?'

She could not restrain a quick glance at the lawyer.

'It must have been about half past eleven.'

'Where were you?'

'In the corridor.'

'The one that goes past your room and his?'

'Yes.'

'You were coming from this drawing-room?'

'No.'

'You were with your husband?'

'No. I had been out by myself.'

'Your husband had remained at home?'

'Yes. He seldom goes out. Especially since he nearly died of pleurisy. He has always been delicate and . . .'

'What time did you go out?'

She asked the lawyer:

'Do I have to answer that?'

'I advise you to, although these questions relate only to your private life and obviously have no connexion whatever with the tragedy.'

'I went out about six o'clock.'

'In the evening?'

'Certainly not at six in the morning.'

'Your lawyer will perhaps allow you to tell us what you did up to half past eleven?'

'I had dinner out.'

'Alone?'

'That's my affair.'

'And then?'

'I went to the cinema.'

'A local one?'

'No, in the Champs-Elysées. When I got back the house was in darkness, at least on the side that overlooks the quay. I went upstairs, into the corridor, and I saw my brother-in-law's door opening.'

'He was waiting for you?'

'I see no reason why he should have been. He usually sat up very late, reading, in the little study next to his room.'

'He came out of the study?'

'Out of his bedroom.'

'How was he dressed?'

'In a dressing-gown. Pyjamas and a dressing-gown. He said:

' "Ah, it's you, Paulette . . ."'

'And I replied:

' "Good night, Léonard.'

' "Good night . . ."'

'That was all.'

'You both went to your rooms?'

'Yes.'

'Did you speak to your husband?'

'I had nothing to say to him.'

'You have communicating rooms?'

'Yes. But the door between them is nearly always shut.'

'And locked?'

The lawyer intervened:

'I think you're going too far, Chief-Inspector.'

The young woman shrugged her shoulders wearily.

'No, not locked,' she said in an off-hand, scornful tone.

'So you didn't see your husband?'

'No. I undressed and got into bed at once.'

'You have your own bathroom?'

'This is an old house. There is only one bathroom on this floor, at the end of the corridor.'

'You went there?'

'I did. Do I have to give you fuller details?'

'Did you notice whether the light in your brother-in-law's room was still on?'

'I saw light under the door.'

'You heard nothing?'

'Nothing.'

'Did your brother-in-law sometimes confide in you?'

'That depends on what you mean by confiding.'

'There are sometimes things that a man would rather talk about to a woman than to his brother or his parents, for instance. A sister-in-law is a member of the family, without being a relative . . .'

She was waiting patiently.

'Léonard Lachaume had been a widower for years; did he talk to you about his affairs with women?'

'I don't even know whether he had any.'

'Did he go out a great deal?'

'Very little.'

'Do you know where he used to go?'

'That was no business of mine.'

'His son is twelve years old, I understand?'

'He was twelve last month.'

'Did Léonard pay much attention to him?'

'The same as any parents who work. Léonard worked hard, and sometimes went down to the office again after dinner.'

'Your mother-in-law is practically helpless, isn't she?'

'She can only walk with a stick, and someone has to help her up and down stairs.'

'Your father-in-law is not very active either?'

'He is seventy-eight years old.'

'So far as I can see, the servant is hardly more sprightly. Yet, unless I am mistaken, the boy's room is on the second floor, in the left wing, with those three old people.'

She began to answer:

'Jean-Paul . . .'

Then, changing her mind, she broke off.

'You were about to say that Jean-Paul, your nephew. . .'

'I've forgotten what I was going to say.'

'How long has he been sleeping on the second floor?'

'Not long.'

'For years? . . . Months? . . . Weeks?'

'About a week.'

Maigret felt certain she had given this information unwillingly, and the lawyer realized it too, for he immediately interrupted.

'Chief-Inspector, I wonder whether you couldn't ask other members of the household for these particulars? Madame Lachaume has had a distressing morning and has not had time to get dressed. I think her husband would be in a better position to . . .'

'In any case, Maître Radel, I have finished with her, at least for the moment. Unless the examining magistrate has any questions to put to her.'

The magistrate made a slight negative gesture.

'I must apologize for keeping you so long, Madame . . .'

'Do you want me to send my husband in?'

'Not at present. I would rather ask a few questions of that old servant, whose name is . . .?'

'Catherine. She has been with my parents-in-law for more than forty years, and she's almost as old as they are. I'll go and see if she's in the kitchen.'

She went out, and the lawyer was on the point of saying something, but thought better of it and lit a cigarette, after tapping it on his silver case.

He had offered one to the magistrate, who had refused, replying:

'No thank you. I don't smoke.'

Maigret, who was thirsty, didn't dare to ask for a drink, and was in a hurry to get out of the house.

A long time went by before they heard a patter of footsteps, followed by a kind of scratching on the door.

'Come in!'

It was old Catherine, who glared at each of them in turn with an even more sombre expression than shortly before, in the study, and then demanded fiercely:

'What do you want with me? And for one thing, if you go on smoking like that in this house, Monsieur Félix will have another attack of asthma.'

What else could one do? Under the sardonic gaze of the magistrate, Maigret, heaving a sigh, laid his pipe down on the little marble-topped table.

3

MORE embarrassed than ever by the magistrate's attitude and by the presence of the lawyer, Maigret began, in the diffident tone of one who is feeling his way:

'I'm told you have been in this house for forty years?'

He thought this would appease her, give her pleasure. Instead of which, she croaked:

'Who told you that?'

And while he was wondering whether their roles were being reversed, so that he would be answering questions from the old woman, she went on:

'It's not forty years I've been here, it's fifty. I took service when my poor lady was scarcely more than twenty and was expecting Monsieur Léonard.'

A rapid calculation. So old Madame La-chaume, who looked the same age as her husband, could hardly be more than seventy. What had the house been like when Catherine, as a little maid doubtless straight up from the country, had arrived in it, to find her young mistress expecting a first baby?

Absurd questions came thronging into Maigret's mind. There must have been an elder Lachaume couple in those days too, another pair of old people, for on the brass plate he had read 'Established in 1817'. Not long after Waterloo.

Perhaps some of the drawing-room furniture had been just where it stood today; the Empire sofa, for instance, that would have been a very handsome piece if they hadn't covered it in garish blue velvet?

Logs must have blazed in all the marble fireplaces. A later generation had put in central heating, which was now no longer used, either to save money or because the boiler was in bad condition.

The stove fascinated him, a little round stove of rusty iron, such as one used to see in small country railway stations and in some government buildings.

Everything had grown seedy, things and people alike. Family and house had withdrawn into themselves and taken on an unfriendly aspect.

Old Catherine let fall a phrase which placed the period more clearly than anything else. Speaking of Léonard as a baby, she announced proudly:

'I nursed him myself!'

So it was not as a servant but as a wet-nurse that she had come to Paris, and Maigret stared, in spite of himself, at her flat chest, her draggling, dirty black skirts.

For she was dirty. Everything here was dirty or grubby, broken, worn, or patched up by the first means to hand.

Because his mind was on these images, Maigret asked a silly question, which Angelot, the young magistrate, doubtless repeated to his colleagues afterwards.

'Did you nurse Monsieur Armand too?'

The retort came pat:

'Where would I have got the milk?'

'The Lachaumes have no other children?'

'Mademoiselle Véronique.'

'She isn't here?'

'Not since a long time.'

'I suppose you heard nothing during the night?'

'No.'

'What time does Monsieur Léonard usually get up?'

'He gets up when he feels like it.'

'Do you know his friends, the people he's in touch with?'

'I've never poked my nose into my masters' private lives, and you'd do well to follow my example. You're here to find the criminal who killed Monsieur Léonard, and not to interfere in the family's concerns.'

Turning her back on him, she made for the dining-room door.

He was on the point of calling her back. But what was the good? If he needed to ask her anything, he would do it when the examining magistrate and the lawyer were not there looking at him in silent jubilation.

He was floundering, true. But he'd be bound to have the last word.

Should he send for old Félix Lachaume, and his semi-paralysed wife? It would have been logical to give them their turn of questioning, but he was afraid of again showing himself, Maigret, not on top of the situation.

The servant had no sooner left the room than he lit his pipe, went out to the landing, where he looked through the window at the long ladder lying across the courtyard. As he had expected, the magistrate and the lawyer followed him.

At least once during his career he had been obliged to work like this, in front of a witness who studied his every move attentively, but on an infinitely less unpleasant case. A certain Inspector Pyke, of Scotland Yard, had obtained permission to follow one of Maigret's cases in order to study his methods, and seldom in his life had Maigret felt so awkward.

People were far too apt to imagine that those celebrated methods were something in the nature of a cookery recipe, laid down once and for all, needing only to be followed to the letter.

'I suppose you intend to question Armand Lachaume?'

It was the lawyer who put this question. Maigret looked at him, undecided, then shook his head.

'No. I'm going to have a look round downstairs.'

'You won't object if I come too? Seeing that my clients . . .'

He shrugged and set off down the stairs of what had once been a handsome, elegant patrician house.

Downstairs, he opened at random a double door, came upon an immense ballroom, plunged in darkness because the shutters were closed. It was stuffy, smelling of mildew. He felt for the electric switch, and two bulbs out of twelve lit up in a chandelier, several of whose festoons of crystal drops were dangling down, broken.

There was a piano in one corner, an ancient harpsichord in another, and carpets rolled up along the walls. In the middle of the floor were piles of magazines, green cardboard files and biscuit-tins.

Though there had once been music and dancing here, no one had set foot in the room for a long time, and the crimson silk that covered the walls had come unstuck in places.

A door stood ajar, opening into a library whose shelves were almost empty, except for red-bound school prizes and a few battered volumes like those in certain of the booksellers' boxes along the quays.

Had the rest been sold? It was more than likely.

49

The furniture as well, no doubt, for there was none left here, except, in a third and even damper room, a billiard table whose green felt top was mouldering.

Maigret's voice sounded strange, as though it came from some vault, when he remarked, speaking more to himself than to the others who were still following him:

'I suppose the offices are on the other side of the entry.'

They went across, heard voices outside on the pavement, where the police were holding back a score or so of inquisitive idlers.

Opposite the ballroom, they at last found a room that was more or less alive, an office that really looked like an office, though still an old-fashioned one. Its walls were panelled, hung with two oil paintings dating from the previous century, and some photographs, the most recent of which presumably represented Félix Lachaume at the age of fifty or sixty. The Lachaume dynasty, in which Léonard's effigy had not yet taken its place.

The furniture was a mixture of Gothic and Renaissance in style, like that which still survives in the head offices of some very old-established businesses in Paris. Tins of various biscuits made by the firm were displayed on shelves.

Maigret knocked on a door, to the right.

'Come in!' called a voice.

They went into a second office, equally old-fashioned but more untidy, where a man of about fifty, with a bald, shiny head, was bent over a ledger.

'I suppose you are the book-keeper?'

'Justin Brême, the book-keeper, yes.'

'Chief-Inspector Maigret.'

'I know.'

Monsieur Angelot, the examining magistrate, and Maître Radel, the family's lawyer.'

'Pleased to meet you.'

'I imagine, Monsieur Brême, that you have heard what happened last night?'

'Sit down, gentlemen. . . '

There was an unoccupied desk facing his own.

'Is this Monsieur Armand Lachaume's desk?'

'Yes, gentlemen. The firm of Lachaume has been a family business for several generations, and not long ago, Monsieur Felix was still working in the next-door office, which his father and grandfather had worked in before him.'

He was stout, rather sallow. Through an open door they could see into a third office, where a man in a grey overall and an elderly typist were at work.

'I'd like to ask you a few questions.'

Maigret pointed to a safe, one of an old type which, despite its size and weight, would not have held out against even a novice among burglars.

'Is it in that safe that you keep the ready cash?'

Monsieur Brême first went and closed the door of the next office, came back, looking embarrassed, glanced at the lawyer as though seeking his advice.

'What ready cash?' he finally inquired, with a sort of wily ingenuousness.

'You employ staff. So you have pay-days. . . .'

'Unfortunately! They come only too often.'

'You must have a cash reserve. . . .'

'I *should* have one, Chief-Inspector! Unhappily we have been living from hand to mouth for a long time now, and this morning there isn't more than ten thousand francs in that safe. Even that will be needed presently, for I have to pay something on account of a bill.'

'Do the employees know about this?'

'They often have to wait several days for their wages, and sometimes they are not paid in full.'

'So it wouldn't occur to any of them to burgle the place?'

Monsieur Brême laughed soundlessly at this idea.

'Certainly not.'

'The local people know how things are?'

'The grocer, the butcher and the dairy woman sometimes call round three or four times for their money . . .'

It was unpleasant to have to see it through. It was like stripping the clothes off someone, and yet it had to be done.

'The Lachaumes have no private fortune?'

'None.'

'How much, in your opinion, might there have been in Monsieur Léonard's pocket-book?'

The book-keeper made a vague gesture.

'Not a lot.'

'Yet the firm keeps going,' objected Maigret.

Monsieur Brême again looked at the young lawyer.

'It seems to me,' the latter intervened, 'that this inquiry is tending more and more to concentrate on my clients instead of on the criminal.'

And Maigret growled:

'You talk like old Catherine, Maître. How do you expect me to trace a murderer unless I discover his motives? We're told he was a burglar . . .'

'The ladder proves it. . . .'

The chief-inspector grunted sceptically:

'Yes! And the disappearance of the pocket-book! And the fact that no weapon has been found yet . . .'

He had not sat down. Neither had the others, despite the suggestion made by the book-keeper, who stood there casting covert glances towards his cushioned chair.

'Tell me, Monsieur Brême, you do pay your employees sooner or later all the same; otherwise they wouldn't go on working. . . .'

'It's a miracle each time.'

'And where does this miraculous money come from?'

The man began to show signs of nervousness.

'Monsieur Léonard used to give it to me.'

'In cash?'

Maître Radel put in:

'You are not obliged to answer, Monsieur Brême.'

'They will find out anyhow, by going through

53

the books or asking the bank. . . . The money is generally given to me in the form of a cheque. . . .'

'You mean Monsieur Léonard had a personal bank account, separate from the firm's account, and that he drew cheques on it when the need became too urgent?'

'No. It was Madame Lachaume.'

'The mother?'

'Madame Paulette.'

At last they were getting somewhere, and Maigret sat down, in satisfaction.

'Sit down at your desk, Monsieur Brême. Take your time to answer me. For how long has Madame Paulette, as you call her, in other words Armand Lachaume's wife, been acting as the good angel of this house?'

'Practically ever since she came into it.'

'When did the marriage take place?'

'Six years ago. Two years after the death of Madame Marcelle.'

'Excuse me, but who was Madame Marcelle?'

'Monsieur Léonard's wife.'

'So it is six years since Armand Lachaume married Paulette . . . Paulette who?'

'Paulette Zuber.'

'She had money?'

'A great deal.'

'Are any of her family still alive?'

'Her father died five months ago and she was his only daughter. As for her mother, she never knew her.'

'Who was Zuber?'

The name was familiar, and he seemed to remember hearing it in some professional connexion.

'Frédéric Zuberski, known as Zuber, the
leather-merchant.'

'He had some trouble, didn't he?'

'The income-tax authorities were hot on his
heels for a time. And after the war it was said
that he . . .'

'Now I've got it!'

Zuberski, who preferred to be called Zuber,
had had his hour of fame. He had started his
career by driving round the countryside in a little
cart, collecting skins and raw-hide from peas-
ants, then he had set up a warehouse, at Ivry,
as it happened, probably not far from Lachaume's.

Even before the war his business was already
doing well and Zuber owned a number of lor-
ries, besides several warehouses in the prov-
inces.

Later on, two or three years after the Liberation, there had been a rumour that he had piled
up a considerable fortune and that his arrest was
imminent.

He had awakened the attention of the Press,
largely because he was such a quaint character:
misshapen, shabbily dressed, speaking French
with a strong foreign accent, and scarcely able
to read or write.

Millions, some people said thousands of millions, of francs passed through his hands, and

he was believed to have a virtual monopoly of the trade in raw-hides, either by direct ownership or through middlemen.

It was not Maigret who had had to deal with him, but the financial branch. In the end the matter had been forgotten and the chief inspector did not know how it had ended.

'What did Zuber die of?'

'Cancer; he was operated on at the Saint-Joseph Clinic.'

'If I understand rightly, it's thanks to his money that the firm of Lachaume keeps more or less afloat?'

'Not exactly. When she married, Madame Paulette brought a considerable dowry. . . .'

'Which she invested in Lachaume's Biscuits?'

'More or less. Let's say it was drawn upon whenever the need arose?'

'And afterwards, when the dowry was all used up? For it was soon used up?'

'Yes.'

'How did they manage after that?'

'Madame Paulette used to go and see her father.'

'Didn't he come here?'

'I don't remember ever seeing him. If he ever came it must have been upstairs, in the evening, but I'm not sure about that.'

'I really do not see what you are trying to get at, Chief-Inspector,' the lawyer protested again.

The magistrate, for his part, seemed keenly interested, and there was even a glint of amusement in his pale eyes.

'Neither do I,' admitted Maigret. 'You see, Maître, at the beginning of an investigation one is in the dark and one can only grope about. So Frédéric Zuber, who had one daughter, gave her in marriage to the younger of the Lachaume sons, Armand, providing her with a comfortable sum by way of dowry. You don't happen to know the exact figure?'

'I protest. . . .'

Radel again, of course; he was on thorns.

'Very well. I'll let that go. The biscuits ate up the dowry. Then, every so often, Paulette was dispatched to see her father, who was not received here. . . .'

'He didn't say that.'

'I will correct myself: who was not received here or who was not a frequent visitor. . . . Old man Zuber used to spit . . .'

It was largely as a protest against the presence of the magistrate and the young lawyer that Maigret took this vulgar tone.

'Then Zuber died. Did the Lachaumes go to his funeral?'

Monsieur Brême smiled wanly.

'That is not my affair. . . .'

'Did you go yourself.'

'No.'

'I suppose there was a marriage settlement? An old fox like Zuber can hardly have . . .'

'They were married under the system of separate property.'

'And a few months ago, Paulette Lachaume inherited her father's fortune. Is that correct?'

'That is correct.'

'So it is she, now, who holds the purse-strings? It is she who must be appealed to when there is no money in the till to settle bills or pay the employees?'

Radel again, as bothersome as a great blue-bottle:

'I don't see where this is getting you.'

'Nor do I, Maître. But neither do I see where I should get to by hunting through Paris for a burglar stupid enough to break into a house where there is no money, using a heavy ladder and smashing a window-pane when there is a glass-panelled door on the ground floor, all this in order to get into the bedroom where a man is asleep, kill him with a noisy revolver, and make off with an almost empty pocket-book.'

'You don't know about that.'

'True enough! Léonard Lachaume may have asked his sister-in-law for money last night. But the fact remains that in this office there is a safe, monumental in size but childishly simple to open, which has not been touched. The further fact remains that when the crime was committed there were at least six people in the house.'

'More puzzling burglaries have been known.'

'Granted. To get into the courtyard where the ladder was standing, somebody had to climb a wall which, if my eyes tell me correctly, is about twelve feet high. Lastly, two people were sleeping within a few yards of the room where the shot was fired, and they heard nothing.'

'We are near a railway line where trains follow one another almost without pause.'

'I am not denying that, Monsieur Radel. My job is to search for the truth, and I am doing so. The mere fact of your presence here would disincline me from searching very far off, for it is unusual, when someone has been murdered, for the relatives to send for a lawyer even before the police have had time to interrogate them.

'I am going to ask you a question you will probably refuse to answer. Armand Lachaume telephoned to you, in my presence, to ask you to come here. Where do you live, Maître?'

'Place de l'Odéon. Very near here.'

'It's true you arrived within ten minutes. You showed no great surprise. You asked very few questions. Are you sure you didn't know before we did what happened last night?'

'I protest vigorously against . . .'

'Against what? I am not, of course, accusing you of entering the house by night, through a window. I am only wondering if you may not have received, early this morning, a previous telephone call, informing you of what had happened and asking your advice. . . .'

'I reserve the full right, in the presence of the examining magistrate, to take any action I may think fit in the light of such an accusation.'

'I'm not accusing you, Maître. I'm only asking. And, if you prefer, I'm asking myself.'

Maigret's hackles were up.

'As for you, Monsieur Brême, I am obliged to

you. I shall probably have to come back and ask you some more questions. It is for the examining magistrate to decide whether these offices should be placed under seal. . . .'

'What do you think?'

He was leaving the decision to Maigret.

'I don't think there would be any point in it, and the books would most likely add nothing to what Monsieur Brême has told us already.'

He looked round for his hat, realized that he had left it upstairs.

'I'll go and fetch it,' the book-keeper proposed.

'Oh, don't trouble.'

Maigret started upstairs, had the feeling of a presence, looked up, and saw Catherine peering down over the banisters. She must have been watching for him.

'Is it your hat you want?'

'Yes. Isn't my inspector up there?'

'He left a long time ago. Catch!'

Without letting him reach the top, she threw his felt hat down at him, and just as he bent to pick it up, she spat.

*

The lawyer had not followed them into the street. Because of the rain that was still falling, as cold and gloomy as it had been all morning, only a few idlers had stayed on, and one uniformed policeman was enough to keep them at a distance. The newspapers, for a wonder, had not yet got wind of the case.

The two black cars, the magistrate's and the one from Police Headquarters, were still parked at the side of the road.

'Are you going back to the Quai des Orfèvres?' asked the magistrate, as he opened his car-door.

'I don't know yet. I'll wait for Janvier, he must be somewhere about.'

'Why do you have to wait for him?'

'Because I can't drive a car,' replied Maigret frankly, pointing to the little police Renault.

'Would you like me to drop you?'

'No thank you. I'd rather wait and sniff the local air.'

He foresaw a risk of searching questions, perhaps even of protests, exhortations to caution and restraint.

'I'd be glad if you would telephone me before midday, Chief-Inspector, to keep me informed. I intend to follow this case very closely.'

'I know. Good-bye for the present.'

The small group of idlers watched them, and a woman hugging a black shawl around her murmured to her neighbour:

'That's the famous Maigret.'

'And who's the young one?'

'I don't know.'

Maigret turned up his coat collar and set out along the pavement. He had scarcely gone fifty yards when someone signed to him from the entrance of a little bar: *Aux Copains du Quai*. It was Janvier.

There was nobody there except the proprietress behind the bar, a fat, tousle-headed woman, watching from a distance, through the kitchen door, over a pot which was steaming on the stove and giving off a strong smell of onions.

'What will you have, Chief?'

Janvier added:

'I had a hot toddy. This is just the weather for catching 'flu.'

Maigret had a toddy too.

'Did you come across anything?'

'I don't know. I thought it might be as well to put seals on the bedroom door before I left.'

'Have you rung up Dr. Paul?'

'He's still on the job. One of his assistants told me they'd found a certain quantity of alcohol in the stomach. They'll ascertain what percentage was in the blood.'

'Nothing else?'

'They've discovered the bullet and are sending it to the expert. The doctor said it was a small calibre, probably a 6.35. What do you think about it yourself, Chief?'

The bar-keeper had gone off to stir her stew with a wooden spoon.

'I preferred this morning's case.'

'The Canon?'

'Chaps like that don't kill people, at any rate.'

'You don't believe their yarn about the burglary?'

'No.'

'Neither do I. The specialists looked for fingerprints on the ladder and the window-pane, but they didn't find any. Except some old prints left on the ladder by the foreman.'

'The fellow might have had gloves on. That doesn't prove anything.'

'I took a look at the outer wall.'

'Well?'

'It's all stuck with broken glass. At one place, not far from the house, some of the glass has been smashed. I had some photos taken.'

'Why?'

'Well, Chief, you know that a cat-burglar makes his plans beforehand. If he knows there's broken glass along a wall, he brings an old sack, or a bit of board. Then you find the glass smashed in a particular way. Whereas here, it had been crushed as though with a hammer.'

'You questioned the neighbours?'

'They didn't hear anything. They all tell me that the trains make an infernal row and that it takes years to get used to them. I noticed there were no shutters on the first- and second-floor windows, so I went to question the crew of the barge you can see unloading over there. I wanted to know if any of them had seen lights in the house after midnight.

'They'd been asleep, as I expected. Those people go to bed early and get up early. But the wife told me one thing that might turn out to be interesting. Last night there was a Belgian barge tied up alongside them, and it left early this morning. It was the *Notre-Dame*, making for the flour-mills at Corbeil.

'Yesterday was the skipper's birthday. Some people from another barge, also a Belgian one, that was moored up-stream, spent part of the night on board the *Notre-Dame*, and one of the chaps had an accordion . . .'

'Have you got the name of the other barge?'

'No. The woman said that must have left, too.'

Maigret called the proprietress, paid for the two drinks.

'Where are we going?' inquired Janvier.

'Drive round the district for a bit. There's something I want to find.'

The little black car had only a few hundred yards to travel along the neighbouring streets.

'Stop. It's here.'

They saw a long wall, full of cracks, an unpaved yard, with buildings, some wooden, some brick-built, which had open-work walls, like those of the store-houses where tobacco is put to dry. Above the entrance was a notice:

F. ZUBER
Leathers and Hides

Below, in more recent paint of a glaring yellow:

David Hirschfeld, Successor

Janvier, who didn't know what this had to do with the case, kept his foot on the clutch.

'The goose that's been laying golden eggs for the Lachaumes for the last six years,' muttered Maigret. 'I'll explain later.'

'Do I wait for you?'

'Yes. I shan't be more than a few minutes.'

He found the office without difficulty, for the word was written above the smallest of the buildings, more like a hut, where a typist was at work beside a stove resembling the one he had just seen in the house on the quay.

'Is Monsieur Hirschfeld here?'

'No. He's at the slaughterhouse. What have you come about?'

He showed his Police Headquarters badge.

'Were you here already in Monsieur Zuber's time?'

'No. I've always worked for Monsieur Hirschfeld.'

'When did Monsieur Zuber sell the business?'

'Just over a year ago, when he had to go into hospital.'

'Did you know him?'

'I typed the deed of sale.'

'Was he an old man?'

'One couldn't put an age to him, because he was already in, and very thin. His clothes hung on him like sacks and his skin was as white as that wall over there. I know he was only fifty-eight.'

'Did you ever meet his daughter?'

'No. I heard about her.'

'In what connexion?'

'When the two men were discussing the sale. Monsieur Zuber had no illusions about his health. He knew he couldn't last more than a few months, a year at the outside. The doctor had told him so straight out. That's why he preferred to make a deed of gift, keeping in his own name only what he needed to pay the hospital and the doctors, which saved a lot in death-duties.'

'Can you tell me the figure?'

'You mean the price Monsieur Hirschfeld paid him?'

Maigret nodded.

'There was so much talk about it in the trade that I don't think I'm being indiscreet. Three hundred.'

'Three hundred what?'

'Millions, of course!'

Maigret couldn't prevent himself from looking round at the scruffy office, the muddy yard, the dilapidated buildings that gave off a disgusting stench.

'And Monsieur Hirschfeld paid that amount cash down?'

She smiled with a touch of pity.

'A sum like that is never paid cash down. He paid part of it. I won't tell you exactly how much, but you can ask him. The rest is to be spread over a period of ten years. . . .'

'The whole lot goes to Zuber's daughter?'

'Yes, in the name of Madame Armand Lachaume. If you'd like to talk to Monsieur Hirschfeld, he's usually back from the slaughterhouse about half past eleven, except on days when he has lunch at La Villette. . . .'

Janvier looked inquisitively at the dreamy, slightly stunned Maigret who returned towards the car, with head bent, and paused on the kerb to fill a pipe.

'Notice a smell here?'

'It stinks, Chief.'

'You see that yard, those huts?'

Janvier waited expectantly.

'Well, my boy, that little lot is worth three hundred million francs. And you know who's getting that three hundred million?'

He slid into his seat, closed the door.

'Paulette Lachaume! Now back to the Quai!'

Until he walked into his office, with Janvier still close behind, he didn't utter another word.

4

M A I G R E T opened the cupboard to hang up his wet coat and hat, caught sight of himself in the mirror above the wash-basin, and nearly put out his tongue, from sheer disgust, at himself. Of course that glass did distort things a bit. But all the same the chief-inspector felt as though he had come back from the Quai de la Gare with a face not unlike those of the people who lived in that weird house.

After so many years in the police force one doesn't, it's true, believe any longer in Father Christmas, in the world as described in improving books and twopence-coloured prints, with the rich on one side, the poor on the other, with the honest people and the scoundrels, the exemplary families gathered, as though at the photographer's, around a smiling patriarch.

But now and then, without realizing it, he

went harking back to childhood memories, and was as much shocked by some things as though he were still a lad.

He had seldom been so shocked as in the Lachaume household. For once, he had really felt he was losing his grip, and even now he still had a kind of bitter aftertaste in his mouth, needed to settle back into his office again, drop heavily into his chair, stroke his pipes, as though to remind himself of the reality of everyday things.

It was one of those days when the lights would be left on all the time, and trickles of rain were zigzagging down the windows. Janvier, who had followed him into the room, was waiting for his instructions.

'Wasn't that Loureau I caught sight of in the corridor?'

Loureau was a journalist who had already been haunting Police Headquarters in the days when Maigret was a mere inspector.

'You might tip him off. . . .'

In the ordinary way he avoided putting the Press on the track at the beginning of a case, for in their eagerness to find everything out at top speed, they are apt to confuse the issue, even to give the alarm to suspects.

It was not a spirit of vengeance against the Lachaumes or against the examining magistrate that prompted him this time to send the journalists to the Quai de la Gare; but in that scaled house where no one said a word and he was forced to go to work with kid gloves on, he felt defenceless, and would not be sorry to see the reporters stirring things up a bit. They didn't have to be as cautious as he did. They weren't saddled with a young magistrate, or with a man like Radel, who would make the hell of a row over the slightest abuse of authority or breach of the regulations.

'Don't give him any details. He'll find those out for himself. After that, come back here.'

He picked up his telephone, asking for the superintendent of police at Ivry.

'Hello? Maigret here. You were kind enough this morning to offer me the help of your inspectors. I shall be very glad of it. I'd like them to look into everything that may have happened around that house during the night. You understand? Particularly between midnight and, say, three in the morning. Perhaps you could find me, in your registers, the present address of Véronique Lachaume, the dead man's sister, who seems to have left the Quai de la Gare home some years ago. Will you give me a ring as soon as you have it? Thank you. Good-bye for the moment.'

He might have summoned Lucas by telephone too, but when he wanted one of the inspectors, he preferred to get up from his arm-chair and go and open the door into their office. It was not to keep an eye on them, but to take the temperature of the place, so to speak.

'Will you come in here for a second, Lucas?'

There were at least six of them in the big room that morning, which was a lot for a Monday.

'How's the Canon?' was his first question after sitting down again at his desk.

'I had him committed.'

'How did it go?'

'Very well. We chatted a bit. You know what I discovered, Chief? In a way he's rather glad someone blew the gaff on him, even if it was his wife. He didn't admit it in so many words, but I could see he'd have been more upset if we'd caught him by our own methods, or because he'd slipped up somehow.'

This was almost refreshing, after the Lachaume household. Maigret wasn't surprised. This was not the first time he had noticed a kind of professional pride among men like the Canon.

'Not that he's exactly pleased to be going to prison, or to discover that it was his wife who gave him away so as to go off for good with another man. But he doesn't grumble, or talk about taking his revenge when he comes out of clink. While he was being weighed and measured, without a stitch on, he gave me a funny look and muttered:

' "Only a silly b— would get married when he's as ugly as I am!" '

Maigret had called Lucas to give him instructions.

'Ring through to Corbeil. Ask their flying squad to send down to the flour-mills and see if the barge Notre-Dame has arrived. If she's not there yet, they'll find her somewhere near the last lock. She tied up last night at the Ivry dock, just opposite the Lachaumes' house. There was a little party on board, and it lasted till very late. Somebody may have noticed lights in the house, or movements around it. There were some other bargemen at the celebration and I want to know their names, the name of their boat, the place where they might be got hold of. You understand?'

'Yes, Chief.'

'That's all, old man.'

Janvier had come back.

'And what am I to do?'

This was the disagreeable period that occurs during every investigation, the moment of uncertainty as to where to turn next.

'Telephone Paul, he must have finished the post-mortem. He may have some extra particulars to give you before he sends in his report. After that, go up to the laboratory. See whether they've found out anything.'

Left alone with his pipes, Maigret selected one of them, the oldest, and filled it slowly, watching the rain trickling down the window-panes.

'Three hundred million! . . .' the words escaped him in a growl, as he saw in his mind's eye the shabby house on the Quai de la Gare, the little stove in the drawing-room, the old furniture which had once been handsome, but had been re-covered in ill-assorted materials, the icy radiators, the great ballroom on the ground floor, the library and the billiard-room, where one expected to see a ghost at any moment.

He called to mind, too, the rather contorted

features of Armand Lachaume, who was obviously a weakling, possibly a coward, and seemed to have lived completely overshadowed by his brother.

'Which of you is free?' he asked, standing in the doorway of the inspectors' office.

Torrence was the first to stand up, as if at school.

'Come into my office, Torrence. Sit down. You're to go to the Quai de la Gare, at Ivry. I'd rather you didn't go into the house, or into the factory or offices. I imagine that at midday the employees, some of them at any rate, go out to lunch.

'Get what you can out of them, and try to make a point of finding the answers to these questions:

'*Firstly:* have the Lachaumes a car, and if so, what make is it?

'*Secondly:* who usually drives it, and was it out last night?

'*Thirdly:* does Paulette Lachaume often go out to dinner? Does anyone know with whom she goes? and have they any idea what she does afterwards?

'*Fourthly:* how do things stand between her and her husband? I can tell you, for what it may be worth, that they have separate rooms.

'*Fifthly:* how did she get along with her brother-in-law? . . .

You've made a note of all that? Lastly, I wouldn't mind knowing who Léonard Lachaume's wife was. She died about eight years ago. Her maiden name. Her family. Was she well off? What did she die of? . . .'

The hefty Torrence was placidly jotting this down in his note-book.

'I think that's all. Naturally it's urgent.'

'I'll go right away, Chief.'

Had he forgotten anything? If the examining magistrate and the lawyer hadn't been there, he would have stayed on at the Quai de la Gare himself and put certain questions direct. He would have liked, too, if only out of curiosity, to take a look at Armand Lachaume's room and still more at his wife's.

Did that heiress, with her three hundred million francs, live as shabbily as the rest of the family?

It was almost noon, and he had promised to telephone to Angelot, the magistrate. He called him up.

'Maigret speaking. I've rung up to report, as you asked me to. There's nothing important to tell you, except that Paulette Lachaume is the daughter of a leather-merchant named Zuber, who left her at least three hundred million francs.'

There was a silence at the other end, then the calm voice of the young magistrate:

'You're certain of that?'

'Practically certain. I shall have the confirmation presently.'

'Has she been long in control of that money?'

'About a year, if my information is correct. When he knew the doctors gave him no hope,

Zuber made a deed of gift to his daughter, so as to avoid death-duties as far as possible.'

'Paulette Lachaume is married under the system of separate property, is she not?'

'That's what we were told this morning. I haven't checked it.'

'Thank you. Please continue to keep me informed. You have nothing else to tell me?'

'My men are busy on routine work.'

He had no sooner rung off than he picked up the telephone again.

'Get me Maître Radel, please.'

This brought the reply that the lawyer was not at his home, where they were waiting for him to return to lunch.

'Ring up the Lachaumes' house on the Quai de la Gare. He may still be there.'

So indeed he was, a fact which set Maigret speculating.

'I have two or three small points to clear up, Maître Radel. As I know you prefer your clients to be disturbed as little as possible, I would rather apply to you. In the first place, what is the name of the Lachaume family's notary . . .?'

'Just a moment. . . .'

There was a fairly long pause, during which the lawyer must have kept his hand carefully over the telephone.

'Hello? Chief-Inspector Maigret? Are you still there? I don't see what you're getting at, but my clients have no objection to my telling you that their notary is Maître Barbarin, Quai Voltaire.'

'I imagine that if Léonard Lachaume left a will, it was with Maître Barbarin that he deposited it?'

'I imagine so too, though I doubt whether a will exists, for the family has said nothing about it.'

'Has Léonard Lachaume's son . . . his name is Jean-Paul, I believe? . . . got back from school yet?'

'One moment, please.'

Another silence. The lawyer's hand was not so squarely over the mouthpiece, and Maigret could hear a hum of voices.

'He will not be coming home. His uncle has arranged, by telephone, for him to remain at school.'

'As a boarder?'

'For the time being, yes. His things will be taken to him presently. Is that all you wish to know?'

'Will you ask Madame Lachaume—junior, of course—the name of her own notary, the one who wound up her father's estate, and probably drew up her marriage settlement?'

This time the silence lasted so long that Maigret wondered whether the man at the other end had not hung up. Only once he heard the voice of the lawyer, who seemed to be angry and was declaring forcibly:

'But I tell you that . . .'

Silence again. Were the Lachaumes putting up a fight? Was Radel trying to convince them that the police would anyhow get to know what they wanted? Who was arguing with the lawyer? Armand Lachaume? His wife? And were the two old people listening to the argument, they who already looked like family portraits?

'Hello? . . . Excuse me, Chief-Inspector. . . . We were interrupted and I couldn't attend to your question at once. . . . Zuber's estate was wound up by his notary, Maître Léon Wurmster, Rue de Rivoli. . . . You got the name? . . . Wurmster . . . Leon. . . . I want to emphasize that, because there's a Georges Wurmster who is a notary at Passy. . . . As for the marriage settlement, Maître Barbarin saw to that. . . .'

'Thank you.'

'Hello? . . . Don't ring off. . . . I am ready to give you any further information you may consider necessary. . . . Contrary to what you may have supposed, my clients have no intention of withholding anything from the police. . . . What would you like to know?'

'First of all, the marriage settlement. . . .'

'Separate properties.'

'Was that all?'

'Madame Lachaume's money to go to her children, if any.'

'And if there were no children?'

'To the survivor of the couple.'

'If I am not mistaken, the sum involved is over three hundred million francs?'

'One moment.'

The silence did not last long.

'There is some exaggeration, but the figure is approximately correct, nevertheless.'

'Thank you.'

'I had the impression there were other points you wished to clear up?'

'Not for the moment.'

He rang up Maître Barbarin, and it took some time to get him, for the notary was at a meeting.

'Chief-Inspector Maigret here. I suppose you already know that one of your clients, Léonard Lachaume, died last night?'

Caught unprepared, the notary answered:

'I have just heard about it.'

'By telephone?'

'Yes.'

'I am not asking you to commit a breach of professional etiquette, but I need to know whether Léonard Lachaume left a will.'

'Not to my knowledge.'

'So he never drew it up in your presence, or left any such document in your office?'

'No. He certainly didn't concern himself with the matter.'

'Why not?'

'Because he owned nothing, except a parcel of shares in Lachaume's Biscuits, and those are valueless.'

'Don't ring off yet, Maître Barbarin. I haven't quite finished. Léonard Lachaume was a widower. Could you tell me the name of his wife?'

'Marcelle Donat.'

He had not needed to look up his files.

'What sort of family did she come from?'

'You've heard of the firm of Donat & Moutier?'

Maigret had often seen these two names on

hoardings and outside building sites. They belonged to a big firm of government contractors.

'Did she have a dowry?'

'Of course.'

'Can you tell me the amount?'

'Not without an order from the examining magistrate.'

'I'll let that go. Considering how wealthy her family is, I presume it was a large sum?'

Silence.

'Did the marriage take place under the system of separate property?'

'My answer is the same as before.'

'And you can't tell me what Madame Léonard Lachaume died of?'

'The family will be able to give you more accurate information than I can as to that.'

'Thank you, Maître.'

Only the background of the picture was beginning to be filled in as yet. Most of the people in it were still hazy, indeterminate, with, here and there, a few features standing out more sharply.

At several years' interval, each of the Lachaume sons, first Léonard, then Armand, had married a rich girl.

Their brides had brought with them dowries, probably large ones, of which nothing apparently remained.

Might it not be these successive contributions that had enabled the once prosperous business, founded in 1817, to survive to the present day?

True, it was tottering on the verge of collapse.

Maigret wondered whether, even in the depths of the country, those packets of wafer-biscuits, with their after-taste of cardboard, could be found nowadays as they were in his childhood.

The two old people, in their drawing-room heated by an iron stove, had practically no individual existence any more; like the billiard-table on the ground floor, like the crystal chandelier, they were merely survivals from the past.

Was not even Armand Lachaume an insubstantial figure, a kind of shadow or partly-faded replica of his brother?

Yet a miracle had happened, had been going on for years; however decayed, the place was still there and smoke still rose from the tall chimney.

The biscuit factory served no purpose, met no standards of business. It had been a thriving, even celebrated concern in the days of small enterprise but now, the market had been won by more up-to-date organizations, two or three of which vied for supremacy in it.

Logically, the biscuit factory on the Quai de la Gare should have closed down long ago.

Whose determination had kept it going in spite of everything?

It was hard to believe that Félix Lachaume was responsible, that dignified, silent old man who no longer seemed fully aware of what was going on around him.

For how long had he been reduced to being merely a kind of ornament?

There remained Léonard. The fact that it was Léonard who was dead to some extent accounted for the family's bewilderment, its reticences, or rather silence, its panic-stricken summoning of a lawyer.

Could one not imagine how, up to last night, it had been Léonard who thought, who *willed* for everybody?

Even for Paulette Lachaume?

That last question was a more perplexing one, and Maigret tried hard to envisage the young woman as he had seen her that morning, tousleheaded, wearing a rather commonplace blue dressing-gown.

His one surprise had been to discover, in that house, amid that family, a young woman who had a certain vitality, even a degree of animal magnetism. He couldn't have said whether she was pretty; but he would have sworn she was desirable.

He would decidedly have liked to see her room, and he wondered whether it was different from the rest of the house.

He wondered, too, how Paulette had come into the place, why she had married such a ludicrous creature as Armand, whose bedroom she did not share.

There were other questions, so many questions, in fact, that he preferred to put off worrying about them.

The telephone rang and he picked up the receiver.

'Maigret here . . .'

It was Lucas.

'I've got Corbeil on the line. They've already questioned the barge people. Shall I put them through to you?'

He assented and heard the voice of an inspector belonging to the Corbeil flying squad.

'I found the *Notre-Dame* in the lock, Chief-Inspector. The skipper and his son have a frightful hangover and don't remember anything much. They were playing, singing, eating and drinking nearly all night.

'Each of them went up on deck at one time or another, to discharge his overflow into the Seine. They paid no attention to what might have been happening on the quay.

'They did notice lights in some of the windows of a big house, but don't know whether it was the one just opposite the barge, or another.

'Their friends' name is Van Cauwelaert and their barge is called the *Twee Gebroeders*; apparently that means the Two Brothers. They're Flemish. They must be unloading somewhere along the Canal Saint-Martin by now. I doubt if they'll be able to tell you much, for at least one of the brothers was so tight that he had to be carried to his own boat.'

'About what time was that?'

'Around four in the morning.'

Once again Maigret opened the door into the next office. Only three inspectors were left in there now.

'Are you very busy, Bonfils?'

'I'm finishing a report, but it's not urgent.'

'Cut along to the Canal Saint-Martin and look for a Belgian barge called the *Twee Gebroeders* . . .'

He completed his instructions and was just back in his office, with his mind bent on lunch, when the telephone rang yet again.

'Torrence here, Chief. I've not got many details yet, but I thought I'd better keep you informed. The Lachaumes have got a car, as well as two old delivery vans and a lorry that's been out of commission for several years. The car is a blue Pontiac, registered under the name of Paulette Lachaume. Her husband doesn't drive. I don't know whether it's true, but people in the district say he's had epileptic fits.'

'Did Léonard ever drive the Pontiac?'

'Yes. He used it as much as his sister-in-law did.'

'Yesterday evening?'

'Paulette didn't take the car. But about six o'clock, when she went out, it was at the door.'

'You don't know whether she left by taxi?'

'I don't know for certain. Most likely she did. From what I'm told she isn't the kind of woman who'd travel by Metro or bus.'

'Did Léonard go out?'

'The Ivry inspectors are dealing with that and questioning the people who live along the quay. According to the men on duty at the time, the blue car was no longer outside the door at eight o'clock. One of them thinks he saw it coming back about ten that evening, but he was some way from the house and didn't see it driven in.'

'Who was at the wheel?'

'He didn't notice. He only remembers a blue Pontiac coming from the direction of Paris and driving towards the quay.'

'That all?'

'No. I have the sister's address. It wasn't easy to get hold of, because she's moved five or six times in the last few years.'

'Did she keep in touch with her family?'

'Apparently not. At the moment she's living in the Rue François Ier, at No. 17, *bis*.'

'Married?'

'I don't think so. Do you want me to go to the Rue François Ier?'

Maigret hesitated, thinking of lunch, of his wife waiting for him at home, then shrugged his shoulders:

'No. I'll attend to that. You keep on poking about down there and ring me every now and then.'

He was curious to meet the third Lachaume, who he anticipated would be unlike the others, since she had been the only one to break away from home.

He put on his still damp overcoat, hesitated whether to take an official car. Like Armand Lachaume, he didn't drive, and he'd have to take someone along with him.

He didn't feel inclined to talk. He went out, and made for the Place Dauphine, knowing that at the last moment he would look in at the *brasserie* for a drink. Some inspectors from other branches were standing at the bar, but none from his own, because they were all out on jobs.

'What will you have, Monsieur Maigret?'

'A toddy.'

Since he'd begun with a toddy he might as well go on, even though this wasn't the time of day for it. The men from the Quai didn't need to watch him for long in order to realize that this was not the moment to speak to him. Some of them even dropped their voices suddenly.

Unconsciously he was trying to fit the occupants of the Ivry house into their places, to imagine them in their daily life, which was not easy.

For instance, they apparently took their meals together. How would a woman like Paulette behave in the presence of the old couple? What was her attitude towards that subdued, withdrawn husband of hers, and towards her brother-in-law, who seemed to be the life and soul of the family?

And in the evenings? . . . Where did they all sit? . . . What did they do? . . . He hadn't seen a wireless or a television set . . .

To run that huge house, though part of it, of course, was left to rack and ruin, there was only one servant, nearly eighty years old.

He mustn't forget the boy, Jean-Paul, whom they'd suddenly pushed into boarding-school but who had so far been coming home every afternoon.

How would a kid of twelve react to that atmosphere?

'Taxi!'

He gave the address in the Rue François Ier and sat back in a corner, still imagining the house at various times of day.

If he had not been dogged by the examining magistrate, he would probably have known more by now. In particular, he had the impression that by questioning Armand Lachaume for long enough, in the right way, he could have made him talk.

'Here we are, sir!'

He paid, looked at the six-storey building in front of which they had stopped. On the ground floor there was a hat shop, and several brass plates bore the names of well-known firms. He went through the main entrance, opened the glass door of a well-kept, almost luxurious lodge. There was not a cat in sight. The place didn't smell of stew, and the concierge was young and prepossessing.

He showed his badge, muttering:

'Chief-Inspector Maigret.'

She at once pointed to a chair upholstered in red velvet.

'My husband has driven you several times and often talked to me about you. He's a taxi-driver. He works at night . . .'

She gestured towards a curtain dividing the lodge from the bedroom.

'He's there. He's asleep . . .'

'You have a tenant called Mademoiselle Lachaume?'

Why did she give that mysterious, amused
smile?

'Véronique Lachaume, yes. You're interested
in her?'

'Has she lived here for long?'

'Wait a minute . . . It's easy, because she re-
newed her lease last month . . . So it must be
just over three years . . .'

'Which floor?'

'The fifth, one of the two flats that have big
balconies.'

'Is she up there now?'

She shook her head and smiled again.

'Does she work?'

'Yes. Not at this time of day.'

Maigret misunderstood her.

'You mean she . . .'

'No. It's not what you're thinking. You know
the *Amazone*, just round the corner in the Rue
Marbeuf?'

Though Maigret knew there was a night-club
of that name, he had never set foot in it. All he
could recollect was a glass-panelled door between two shop-fronts, a neon sign, and some
photographs of scantily clad women.

'Does that place belong to her?' he queried.

'Not exactly. She's the barmaid and hostess.'

'The clientele is a bit unusual, isn't it?'

This seemed to amuse the concierge considerably.

'I don't think many men go there. But there are women in dinner-jackets . . .'

'I understand. That being so, Mademoiselle Lachaume presumably isn't home much before four in the morning?'

'Five o'clock, half past five . . . She used to be very regular. For some months now, there've been times when she hasn't come home at all. . . .'

'Is she having an affair?'

'A proper one, with a man.'

'Do you know who he is?'

'I can tell you what he looks like: a fellow of about forty, smartly dressed, who drives a Panhard convertible.'

'Does he sometimes spend part of the night up there?'

'He has done two or three times. More often it's she who goes to his place.'

'You don't know where he lives?'

'I'm pretty certain it can't be far. Mademoiselle Véronique, as I call her, goes everywhere by taxi. She doesn't like the Metros or buses. But when she's spent the night out I see her coming home on foot, so I take it she hasn't far to come.'

'You don't remember the number of the Panhard?'

'It begins with seven-seven . . . I'd almost bet it ends with a three, but I'm not positive . . . Why? . . . Is it urgent?'

At the beginning of an investigation everything is urgent, for one never knows what unexpected developments there may be.

'She has the telephone?'

'Of course.'

'What's the flat like?'

'Three fine rooms and a bathroom. She's furnished it in very good taste. I'm pretty certain she earns a very good living.'

'Is she a pleasant woman?'

'You mean, is she pretty?'

The concierge's eyes twinkled again.

'She's thirty-four and makes no bones about it. She's fat, with about twice as much bosom as me. Her hair's cut short, like a man's, and when she goes out she always wears a suit. Her features are rather heavy, and yet she's attractive, perhaps because she's always in a good temper and doesn't seem to have a care in the world.'

Maigret was beginning to understand better why the youngest of the Lachaumes had been in a hurry to leave her ancestral home.

'Before this latest affair you told me about, did she have any others?'

'Fairly often, but they never lasted. She would sometimes bring a man back with her at five in the morning, as I told you. Regularly, about three o'clock in the afternoon, I'd see a man leaving, keeping his face turned away and slinking close along the wall . . .'

'In other words this is her first real liaison since she came to live here?'

'That's what I think.'

'Does she seem to be in love?'

'She's gayer than ever. Draw your own conclusions.'

'You don't know at what time I'd be likely to find her at home?'

'Anything's possible. She may come back late in the afternoon, or she may equally well go straight to the night-club without looking in here. That's happened two or three times. Don't you think I ought to wake my husband? If he finds out that you've been here and that he missed you . . .'

Maigret pulled out his watch.

'I'm in a hurry, but I'm sure to be round again.'

A few minutes later he was standing in front of the women's photographs displayed at the entrance of the *Amazone*. The iron-barred door was shut and there was no bell.

An errand-boy cast an ironic glance over his shoulder at the elderly gentleman who seemed to be rapt in the contemplation of suggestive photographs, and Maigret, noticing this, moved away with a growl.

5

I N actual fact—as his wife must have suspected long ago—if Maigret seldom went home for meals when he was in the thick of an investigation, it wasn't so much to save time as to remain withdrawn into himself, so to speak, like a sleeper who curls up when morning comes, swathed in his bedclothes, to get his own smell into his nostrils.

It was the private lives of other people, in reality, that Maigret was sniffing up, and at this moment, for instance, in the street, with his hands in the pockets of his overcoat, the rain on his face, he was still lost in the bewildering atmosphere of the Quai de la Gare.

Was it surprising that he should be reluctant to go home, back to his flat, his wife, his furniture, to a kind of unchanging order that had no connexion with the more or less degenerate Lachaumes?

This withdrawal into his shell, and certain other tricks, such as his legendary grumpiness at such times, his hunched shoulders, his gruff manner, were all part of a technique that he had unconsciously built up as the years went by.

For example, it was not merely by chance that he finally went into an Alsatian *brasserie*, where he took a table near the window. He needed to feel solid ground under his feet, that afternoon. He wanted to be weighty, impervious.

He was glad to find that the waitress, in her regional costume, was sturdy and healthy-looking, with a laughing, dimpled face and curly fair hair, unburdened with any psychological complexities. Following the same train of thought, he found it natural to order a *choucroute*, which in this place was lavish and plentifully garnished, accompanied by shiny sausages and fresh pink pickled pork.

After giving his order—including the traditional beer—he went to telephone to his wife, who betrayed her curiosity only by three short questions.

'A murder?'

'Something of the kind.'

'Where?'

'Ivry.'

'Difficult?'

'I think so.'

She did not ask whether he would be home

for dinner, for she knew beforehand that it might be a day or two before she set eyes on him again.

He ate abstractedly, tossed off two big mugs of beer, drank his coffee while watching the rain that was still slanting down, almost horizontally, and the passers-by who bent forward as they walked and held their umbrellas like shields in front of them.

He had forgotten his stiff neck. It must have worn off as he moved about. When he got back to his office, a little after two o'clock, there were several messages waiting for him.

He took time to make himself comfortable, to fill a fresh pipe, and remembering the little iron stove at the Quai de la Gare he regretted the almost identical stove he had kept in his office long after central heating had been put in at the Quai des Orfèvres, which the powers that be had finally taken away from him.

For years people had laughed about the way he was always poking that stove; it was because he liked to see the shower of falling sparks, just as he liked the booming sound the thing made at every gust of wind.

The first message he looked at was from one of the Ivry inspectors. A certain Mélanie Cacheux, housewife, who lived next door to the Lachaumes, had been to visit her sister in the Rue Saint-Antoine the evening before. She had dined there and come home by Metro at about nine o'clock.

As she drew near her home, she had seen the

blue Pontiac outside the biscuit factory. Léonard Lachaume was opening the double doors, and while she hunted in her bag for her key, he had got back into the car and driven it through to the courtyard.

She had not spoken to him, for though she had been living on the quay for fifteen years she was not acquainted with the Lachaumes and knew them only by sight.

The inspector had asked her if she was sure of this. Mélanie Cacheux had been quite positive it was Léonard, the elder of the sons. She had added what Maigret already knew:

'Besides, his brother never drives the car.'

Had Léonard Lachaume gone out again later?

Not for the time being, at any rate. The woman lived on the first floor. Her flat overlooked the quay. She had taken the opportunity of her outing to air it. When she got in she had gone straight to the window and had heard the neighbours' heavy double doors being closed, with a familiar squeak of bolts. She had automatically glanced down at the pavement and there had been nobody in sight.

The second note was from Inspector Bonfils, whom Maigret had sent to the Canal Saint-Martin. He had found the boat, the *Twee Gebroeders*, which was unloading bricks. Bonfils had had to visit several *bistrots* before finding one of the two brothers, Jef Van Cauwelaert, who seemed disposed to continue the previous night's festivities.

Jef had gone up on deck several times during

the evening and night. It was his brother, not he, who was playing the accordion. On one occasion he had heard a noise on the quay. A peculiar sound, which had caused him to look up while he was relieving his bladder:

'As though someone was smashing glass, see what I mean?'

It came from the wall of the biscuit factory. There was no one on the pavement, or beside the wall.

Yes, he was sure he had caught sight of a head projecting above it, the head of someone in the yard, who must have been standing on a ladder.

How far from the house? About ten yards. And at that time Jef Van Cauwelaert had not had more than five or six glasses of gin.

Maigret turned to the plan drawn up by the Judicial Identity people. The spot where the broken glass had been crushed, on the top of the wall, was marked by a cross, twelve yards or so from the house. Now there was a street-lamp less than three yards away, which added plausibility to the bargeman's statement.

Bonfils had emphasized the question of the time, wanting to make sure that it had not been during one of the man's other visits to the deck that he had witnessed the incident.

'It's easy to find out, because they hadn't cut the cake yet.'

Bonfils had gone back on board the barge to ask Jef's wife. The cake had been cut about half past ten.

Maigret registered this in his mind, without

attempting to fit the particulars into place and draw conclusions from them.

He glanced over a third message, again from Ivry, later by a few minutes than the first. These scraps of paper, none of them bearing more than a few lines, each represented hours of going round in the rain, and an impressive number of people who had been asked what appeared to them to be ridiculous questions.

At six o'clock on the previous evening—working backwards—a certain Madame Gaudois, who kept a little grocery just opposite the Pont National, had seen a red sports car parked a few yards away from her shop. She had noticed that the windscreen-wipers were working and that a man was seated at the wheel. The man had switched on the inside lamp and was reading a newspaper. He seemed to be waiting for someone.

The car had stood there for a long time. Counting how many customers she had served while it was there, Madame Gaudois estimated that it must have waited for about twenty minutes.

No. The man was not very young. About forty. He was wearing a yellow raincoat. She had seen him more clearly when, growing impatient, he had got out of the car and begun to walk up and down the pavement. At one time he had even come and looked in the window of the grocery.

He wore a brown hat. He had a little moustache.

It wasn't one of the Lachaumes; neither Monsieur Léonard nor Monsieur Armand. She knew them both by sight. Not to mention that old Catherine sometimes bought things from her, and owed her money. Those people had a trail of bills in every shop in the district.

The keeper of the grocery had heard the footsteps of a woman walking in high-heeled shoes. The lamp in a shop window lit up part of the pavement, and she was sure it had been Paulette Lachaume who had joined the man, even to the point of describing her as wearing a fur coat and a beige hat.

The man in the driving-seat had opened the door. Paulette Lachaume had stooped to get in, because it was a very low car.

'You don't know what make it was?'

She knew nothing about makes. She had never owned a car. She was a widow and . . .

The inspector's professional conscience had impelled him to bring her a sheaf of prospectuses with pictures of different cars.

'It was like that one!' the grocer had said, pointing to a Panhard.

That was all, except an afternoon paper in which Lucas had ringed a short snippet with a blue line:

BURGLAR'S CRIME

Last night, a burglar broke into a house on the Quai de la Gare at Ivry, occupied by the Lachaume family. Léonard Lachaume, the elder son of the family, caught him in the act, but was shot in doing so.

It was not until this morning that the family found the body and. . .

Details would come later. By this time there must be at least a dozen journalists prowling round Ivry.

Maigret sat placidly in his office, where the smoke from his pipe was beginning to form a blue cloud on a level with his forehead, and sorted out this information.

At six o'clock, which corroborated what they already knew, Paulette Lachaume left the house on the quay, wearing a fur coat and a beige hat. She did not take her own car, but hurried off on foot to the Pont National, some two hundred yards away, where a man was waiting for her in a red sports car which seemed to have been a Panhard.

At about the same hour, her own car, the blue Pontiac, was parked outside the biscuit factory.

There was no precise information as to the time at which that car had been used.

All that was known was that towards seven o'clock it was no longer there, and that around nine o'clock Léonard Lachaume brought it back and ran it into the garage at the far end of the courtyard.

What time did the Lachaumes have dinner? In the ordinary way there should be six of them at table, because young Jean-Paul was not yet a boarder at his school.

Paulette was definitely out that evening. Léonard too, almost certainly.

So in the dining-room there were only the two old people, Armand, and the boy.

At about ten o'clock the bargeman belonging

to the *Twee Gebroeders* heard the sound of glass being smashed on the top of the wall, and caught sight of a face.

At half past eleven Paulette came home, by some unknown means. Had she taken a taxi? Or had the red car brought her back?

While she was going down the first-floor corridor, her brother-in-law, in pyjamas and dressing-gown, half-opened his door and wished her good-night.

Was Armand already asleep then? Had he heard his wife come in?

Once undressed, Paulette had gone to the general bathroom, at the far end of the corridor, and had noticed a streak of light under Léonard's door.

Then, as was her custom, she would have taken a sleeping-drug, and apparently slept until morning without hearing anything.

The rest was more in the nature of conjecture, except the time of Léonard's death, which Dr. Paul put between two and three in the morning.

When and where had he drunk the fairly considerable quantity of alcohol revealed by the examination of the stomach and by the blood-analysis?

Maigret turned to the experts' first report. It included a meticulous inventory of everything in the dead man's room, with a description of the furniture, hangings and miscellaneous objects. There was no mention of a bottle or a glass.

'Get me Dr. Paul, please. He's pretty sure to be at home at this time of day.'

So he was, just returned from a lunch out, which had put him into an excellent temper.

'Maigret here. I wonder if you could clear up one point for me. It's about the alcohol found in Léonard Lachaume's body.'

'In the stomach, at any rate, it was brandy,' replied Paul.

'What I would like is to get some idea of the time at which he drank it. Do you know at all?'

'I could even fix it to within half an hour by scientific methods, for the organism eliminates alcohol at a regular rate, though the rate does vary slightly from one individual to another. Some of the alcohol found in the blood was drunk early in the evening, perhaps before that, but only a comparatively small proportion. The brandy that was still in his stomach when he was killed had been drunk quite a long time after his last meal; to leave a safe margin, I would say between eleven in the evening and one o'clock at night. If you want me to tell you how much he'd drunk, I'd rather not commit myself quite so positively, but I should put it not far short of half a pint.'

Maigret remained silent for a moment, digesting this information.

'Is that all you wanted to know?'

'Just a moment, Doctor. Would you say from the post-mortem that Léonard was a heavy drinker, or even a habitual drunkard?'

'Neither one nor the other. His liver and arteries were in perfect condition. The only thing I discovered was that he'd had a touch of TB in his childhood, perhaps without knowing it, a thing that happens more often than people imagine.'

'Thank you, Doctor.'

Léonard Lachaume had left the house on the quay at some undetermined hour, in any case later than his sister-in-law, since the Pontiac was still drawn up by the kerb when she had gone off to join an unknown man.

He might have gone out immediately after her, or not until later. At all events he had come home at nine o'clock.

The household would not all have gone to bed by that hour. What about young Jean-Paul, for instance? It wasn't certain. And it was unlikely that Léonard would have gone to his room without looking into the drawing-room first.

So there had been an encounter between him, his brother and the old couple, at any rate some sort of meeting of uncertain duration, while Catherine was busy in the kitchen, washing up.

Had Léonard begun to drink at that stage already? What had they talked about? When had his parents gone up to bed on the floor above?

If it hadn't been for the zeal and doggedness of Angelot, the examining magistrate, who had prevented him from questioning the family as he would have liked to do, Maigret would doubtless have known all this by now.

Had the two brothers been left to each other's company? What did they do at such times? Did each of them sit reading in opposite corners of the room? Or did they chat?

It wasn't in his own room that Léonard had drunk the brandy, for neither glass nor bottle had been found there.

Either Armand had gone to bed first, leaving his elder brother in the drawing-room, or the latter had come back there later on.

Léonard was not a drunkard. Paul, who had cut up thousands of corpses in the course of his career, was positive, and Maigret had learnt to rely on him.

Yet between eleven at night and two in the morning, the elder Lachaume had drunk roughly half a pint of brandy.

Where was drink kept, in the house? In some drawing-room or dining-room cupboard? Had Léonard been obliged to go down to the cellar?

At eleven-thirty or midnight he was in his room, when his sister-in-law had returned home.

Had he been drinking already? Or hadn't he begun until after that?

Various inspectors, at least ten of them, were still going around in the rain, ringing doorbells, questioning people, trying to jog their memories.

Other particulars would gradually be added to those Maigret already possessed, confirming or conflicting with previous ones.

He was just feeling inclined to get up and stroll into the inspectors' room to change his train of thought, when the telephone rang.

'There's a Madame Boinet on the line, who says she must speak to you personally.'

The name meant nothing to him.

'Ask her what it's about.'

Because his name appeared with undue frequency in the papers, complete strangers were always insisting that they must speak to him personally, even on subjects that had nothing to do with him, such as a lost dog or the renewal of the passport.

'Hello? She says she's the concierge from the Rue François Iᵉʳ.'

'Put her through to me. . . . Hello? . . . Good afternoon, Madame. . . . Maigret here.'

'It isn't easy to get hold of you, Chief-Inspector, and I was afraid they wouldn't give you a message. I wanted to tell you she's just come in.'

'By herself.'

'Yes, loaded with provisions, which means she'll be having dinner at home.'

'I'll be right round.'

Again he decided to take a taxi, rather than one of the black Police Headquarters cars, which were too well known. It was beginning to get dark. He was delayed by two traffic blocks in the Rue de Rivoli, and it took ten minutes to cross the Place de la Concorde, where the wet roofs of the cars seemed to be practically touching one another.

As soon as he entered No. 17 *bis*, the concierge peeped out of her door.

'Fifth door, on the left. I can tell you already that among the things she brought back there were some leeks.'

He gave her a conspiratorial wink, but did not go into the lodge, for he had caught sight of the

103

husband and did not want to waste time chatting.

The house was prosperous-looking, the lift slow but silent. On the fifth floor there was no name on the left-hand door, and Maigret pushed the bell, heard footsteps coming from some distance, muffled by a carpet.

The door was opened eagerly. It was not he who was expected. The woman who received him frowned slightly, as though trying to remember his face.

'Aren't you . . . ?'

'Chief-Inspector Maigret.'

'I was sure I'd seen your face somewhere. I thought at first it was at the cinema, but it was in the papers. Come in.'

Maigret was surprised, for Véronique Lachaume bore only a distant resemblance to the concierge's description of her. True, she was buxom, even fat, to be frank, but she was wearing a dainty housecoat, not a mannish suit, and the room into which she led him was more like a boudoir than a living-room.

Everything was white, the walls, the satin-covered furniture, except for a touch of blue provided by some pieces of china and the old rose colour of the thick-piled carpet, a colour scheme that was reminiscent of a picture by Marie Laurencin.

'What are you surprised about?' she inquired, indicating an arm-chair.

He was afraid to sit down, because of his damp overcoat.

'Take off your coat and give it to me.'

She went to hang it up in the hall. The concierge had been right about one thing, at least: an appetizing smell of leeks was already coming from the kitchen.

'I hadn't expected the police to be here so quickly,' she remarked, sitting down opposite Maigret.

Instead of making her plain, her plumpness rendered her attractive and very likeable, and Maigret suspected that a lot of men must find her desirable. She didn't simper, didn't even bother to fold her house-coat over a considerable stretch of bare leg.

Her feet, with their painted toenails, played in and out of a pair of white mules trimmed with swansdown.

'You may smoke your pipe, Chief-Inspector.'

She took a cigarette from a case, got up to fetch matches, sat down again.

'What rather surprises me is that the family should have told you about me. You must have bombarded them with questions to induce them to do so, because they look upon me as the black sheep, and I imagine my name is taboo in the household.'

'You know what happened last night?'

She pointed to an open newspaper lying on a chair.

'I only know what I've just read.'

'You looked through the paper when you got back here?'

She hesitated only for a second.

105

'No. At my friend's flat.'

She added good-humouredly:

'I'm thirty-four, you know; I'm a big girl now.'

Her full bosom, scantily covered by the white frills, seemed almost to have a life of its own and to quiver in sympathy with her mood. Maigret would have been inclined to call it a gay, good-natured bosom rather than a voluptuous one.

Her eyes were prominent, bright blue in colour, shrewd and innocent at the same time.

'You're not too surprised that I didn't rush off to the Quai de la Gare? I must admit I probably shan't go to the funeral. I wasn't invited to my brothers' weddings, nor to the funeral of my first sister-in-law. I wasn't told when my nephew was born. It's a complete break, as you see!'

'Didn't you want it to be like that?'

'It was I who left home, yes.'

'For some definite reason? If I'm not mistaken, you were eighteen at the time.'

'And the family wanted to marry me to a dealer in non-ferrous metals. Mark you, even without that, I should have left, though a bit later, perhaps. Have you been down there?'

He nodded.

'I don't suppose it's changed for the better? As sinister as ever? What surprises me most is that the burglar wasn't scared. Either he was drunk, or he hadn't seen the house by daylight.'

'You believe in the burglar?'

'The newspaper . . .' she began.

Her brow wrinkled.

'Isn't that true?'

'I'm not sure. Your family isn't talkative.'

'I can remember times, when I was a girl, when they'd spend a whole evening without opening their mouths a dozen times. What's my sister-in-law like?'

'Rather pretty, so far as I could judge.'

'Is it true she's very rich?'

'Very.'

'Do you understand why that is?'

'I hope I shall end by understanding everything.'

'I read what the papers said about her at the time of the marriage. I saw some photos. I felt sorry for the poor girl, then I began to wonder.'

'What conclusion did you come to?'

'If she'd been ugly it would have been easier. Perhaps it was her father who put me on the track, in the end. He'd had difficulties, hadn't he? He started at the bottom. They say that in the beginning he drove his own trap from one farm to another, and that he couldn't read or write. I don't know whether his daughter went to a convent. Whatever school she went to, convent or not, the girls must have given her a hard time of it.

'To some people, especially at Ivry, the name of Lachaume still sounds impressive. That house on the quay remains a kind of fortress. You see what I mean?

'Those Zubers, father and daughter, jumped into the upper middle class at one go. . . .'

Maigret had thought of this.

'I suspect she's paying a high price for it,' she went on. 'Won't you have a drink?'

'No, thank you. You haven't seen any member of your family again recently?'

'Not one.'

'You've never been back there?'

'I'd rather go out of my way not to set eyes on the house; it's left me too many unpleasant memories. Though my father is probably a good sort. It isn't his fault that he was born a Lachaume and it's turned him into what he is now.'

'What about Léonard?'

'Léonard was much more of a Lachaume than Father. It was Léonard who was determined to make me marry the metal-dealer, a frightful creature, and he used to talk to me about the marriage in the tone of a king explaining to his children that it was their duty to carry on the dynasty.'

'Did you know your first sister-in-law?'

'No. In my time, my brother, in spite of his efforts, hadn't yet found an heiress for himself. I was to be the first to be asked to sacrifice myself. As for Armand, he was an invalid in those days. He's never been strong. But even when he was still only a boy he was a bad copy of Léonard. He'd go to great trouble imitating his movements, his bearing, his voice. I used to make fun of him. He's rather pathetic, really. . . .'

'You have no idea what can have happened last night?'

'None at all. Remember, I know less about it than you do. Was it really not a burglar?'

'I'm beginning to doubt it more and more.'

'You mean you think the crime was committed by someone inside the house?'

She pondered for a moment, and her conclusion was unexpected, to say the least of it:

'That's priceless!'

'Why?'

'I don't know. It takes a bit of courage to kill someone and I don't see who, in my family . . .'

'Where were you last night?'

She was not offended.

'It's surprising, now I come to think of it, that you didn't ask me that before. I was behind the bar of the *Amazone*. I take it you know about that? That's probably why you seemed astonished to find me in the kind of get-up the magazines call 'frothy'. The *Amazone* is my work. Black velvet dinner-jacket and monocle. Here, I'm me. See what I mean?'

'Yes.'

'When I'm at home I tend to exaggerate in the opposite direction, a kind of revenge for having to spend part of my time pretending to be a masterful woman.'

'You even have a lover.'

'I've had lots. I'll tell you something that caused a bit of a stir in the family at the time, and helped me to make up my mind: at the age of sixteen I was the mistress of my drawing-master. I had no choice, he was the only man who taught at my school.'

'It's never happened for one of your brothers, or your sister-in-law, to turn up at the *Amazone*?'

'To begin with, I don't suppose they know I work there, since I never gave them my address, and I'm not well known except in a small and rather specialized circle. Secondly, I doubt whether they'd be keen on seeing a member of the La-chaume family behind the bar of a night-club. But . . .'

She hesitated, not sure of herself.

'I don't actually know my sister-in-law Pau-lette. And her photo hasn't been in the papers for years, not since the wedding. One evening I had the impression I recognized her at one of the tables, but it was only a vague impression, that's why I hesitated to mention it. What struck me was the way that woman stared at me, with a curiosity that's difficult to account for. There was also the fact that she was alone.'

'When did this happen?'

'Six weeks ago, two months perhaps.'

'You haven't seen her again?'

'No. Do you mind if I go and take a look at my soup?'

She stayed for some little time in the kitchen, whence he could hear the sound of pans, plates and forks being moved.

'I took the chance of putting the joint into the oven. You mustn't tell this to the proprietress of the *Amazone*, or the clients, because they'd stop taking me seriously and I might lose my job, but I adore cooking.'

'Just for yourself?'

'For myself and sometimes for two.'

'This evening it's for two?'

'How did you guess?'

'You just mentioned a joint.'

'So I did. My friend will be here presently.'

'It's a serious affair this time, isn't it?'

'Who's been telling you that? One of the girls at the *Amazone*? Not that it matters, for I don't hide it. Well, Chief-Inspector, just imagine, at the age of thirty-four I've fallen in love and I've half a mind to throw up everything and get married. I enjoy housekeeping, marketing, going to the butcher's and the dairy. I like staying at home and cooking tasty things. All that becomes far and away more delightful if one's expecting somebody and laying the table for two. So . . .'

'Who is it?'

'A man, of course. Not young. Forty-four. Just the right difference in age. Not specially handsome either, but not ugly. On his side, he's tired of furnished rooms and restaurants. He's an advertising agent. He chiefly handles film advertising, so he's obliged to go every day to *Fouquet's*, *Maxim's*, *the Elysée Club*. . . .

'He's had all the starlets he wanted, but they too live mostly in hotels and eat at restaurants.

'So he's beginning to think that a woman like me . . .'

Beneath the surface irony it was clear that she was in love, perhaps passionately.

'I've just come back from his place, and we shall be having dinner alone here presently. It's time I laid the table. If you have any more questions to ask, come along with me. I can work while I'm listening and answering. . . .'

111

'I'd just like you to give me his name and address.'

'You need him?'

'It's unlikely.'

'Jacques Sainval, 23 Rue de Ponthieu. Jacques Sainval isn't his real name. He's actually Arthur Baquet, but that's too ordinary-sounding for an advertising man. So he adopted a pseudonym.'

'Thank you very much.'

'What for?'

'For receiving me so nicely.'

'Why shouldn't I? You wouldn't even have a drink! As a matter of fact I haven't got much here in the flat. I'm obliged to drink champagne all night, and that's quite enough. Most of the time I just take a sip or two and empty the rest down the sink.'

Here was a woman still getting fun out of life.

'You mustn't be shocked that I've not been weeping. I should have, perhaps, but I can't manage it. I'm longing to know who killed Léonard.'

'So am I.'

'You'll tell me?'

'I promise.'

It was rather as though the two of them had become fellow-conspirators, for Maigret, as he left, was smiling almost as light-heartedly as the plump young woman in her rustling housecoat.

He stood alone on the landing, waiting for the lift, and when it came up there was someone in it, a man with brown hair, starting to thin at the temples.

He was wearing a light-coloured raincoat, with a brown felt hat in his hand.

'Excuse me . . .' he murmured, as he went past the chief-inspector.

Then he turned back for a better look, as though he, too, found the face familiar.

The lift went down. The concierge was on the watch, behind her glass-panelled door.

'Did you see him? He's just gone up.'

'Yes.'

'What do you think of her?'

'She's charming.'

He thanked her and smiled. He might need her again and he mustn't discourage her. He also shook hands with the taxi-driver husband, who had driven him several times.

When at last he emerged on the pavement, he saw a red Panhard convertible outside the door.

6

I t was a little time before Maigret could thread
his way across between the cars, for this was
the after-office rush-hour. On reaching the opposite pavement, he looked up at the flat he had
just left. The balcony ran the hole width of the
house, divided half-way along by a wrought-
iron fence. It was quite dark now, and light was
shining through at least half of the curtained
windows.

The french windows on the fifth floor stood
half-open, and a man with a cigarette in his
mouth, who was leaning on the balcony rail to
look down into the street, drew back hastily when
he saw the chief-inspector.

It was the one who had just gone up and who
had frowned when he passed Maigret at the
door of the lift, the man who called himself

Jacques Sainval and whose business was cinema advertising.

He had gone back into the flat. The french window was closing now. What would he be saying to Véronique Lachaume, as she laid the table?

There was a bar opposite the block, not a *bistrot*, but one of those American bars with high stools and soft lighting that are becoming more and more numerous in the Champs-Elysées district.

Maigret went in; the place was crowded, but he found a stool by the wall. It was hot. There was a lot of noise, women's laughter, cigarette-smoke. A pretty girl in a black dress and white apron waited, smiling, to take his coat and hat.

When the barman turned his way, also looking as if he were wondering where he'd seen him before, Maigret hesitated briefly before ordering:

'A hot toddy!'

Then he inquired:

'The telephone?'

'In the basement.'

'Can you give me a *jeton*?'

'See the girl at the switchboard.'

It wasn't the sort of spot he went to for choice, and he felt, as usual, a bit out of place there, for in his young days such bars hadn't existed. The wooden panelling on the walls was painted with hunting scenes full of pink-coated riders, and a real hunting-horn was hanging just above the bar.

As he made for the stairs at the far end of the room, he could feel himself being stared at. The barman had finally recognized him. So, probably, had others. Most of the women were young. The men, though rather older, didn't belong to his generation.

He too had noticed several familiar faces, and he remembered that there were some television studios just up the street.

He went down the oak staircase, found another pretty woman sitting in front of a telephone switchboard near the cloakroom door.

'A *jeton*, please.'

There were three glass-fronted cabins, but the telephones inside were without dials.

'What number do you want?'

He was obliged to give the number of Police Headquarters, and the young woman recognized it herself, and looked more closely at Maigret.

'Cabin 2.'

'Police Headquarters.'

'Maigret speaking. Would you put me on to Lucas?'

'One minute, Chief-Inspector. . . .'

He had to wait, Lucas was already speaking to someone. At last his voice came over the line.

'I'm sorry, Chief. As it happens, that was the examining magistrate. He called up for the third time since you left, and he's surprised at getting no news from you.'

'Go on.'

'He asked me a whole lot of questions. . . .'

'What about?'

'He began by asking whether you'd been back to the Quai de la Gare. . . . I said I thought not. . . . He wanted to know whether you'd interrogated any other witnesses. . . . Finally, a few minutes ago, he left a message for you. . . . He has to go home to change, because he's dining out. . . . He'll be all the evening at Balzac 23.74. . . .'

This was in the Champs-Elysées district, where Maigret was now.

'He insisted that if you planned to question anybody, he particularly wanted it to be done in his office. . . .'

Lucas was clearly embarrassed.

'Is that all?'

'No. He asked me where the inspectors were, what they were doing, what they'd found out. . . .'

'Did you tell him?'

'No. I made out I didn't know anything. He wasn't pleased.'

'Is there any news?'

Through the glass door he could see the switchboard operator watching him while she put on lipstick, and a woman customer adjusting her suspenders in front of a mirror.

'No. Lapointe has just come on duty. He's getting impatient. He'd love to have something to do.'

'Let me speak to him.'

This was a stroke of luck.

'Lapointe? Take one of the cars and go to Ivry. At the corner of a street just opposite the Pont National, you'll see a badly-lit grocery. I've forgotten the woman's name. Something like Chaudais, Chaudon, or Chaudois . . . She wears her hair in a bun and has one eye a bit askew. Be very nice to her, very polite.

'Tell her we need her for a short time. She'll want to dress up in her best. Try not to let her take too long about it. Then bring her to the Rue Francois Ier, opposite No. 17 *bis*. You'll most likely see a red car parked outside. Pull up as close to it as you can. Stay in the car, both of you, till I get in touch with you. . . .'

'Right, Chief.'

He went out of the cabin, paid for the call.

'Thank you, Monsieur Maigret.'

That had long ago ceased to thrill him. There were more people in the bar upstairs by this time, and a red-headed young woman had to draw aside so that he could get back on his stool. He could feel her warm thigh against his, and she was using very strong scent.

At one table a man of his own age, with grizzled hair and a balding head, had his arm round the waist of a dimpled girl hardly twenty years old, and Maigret, for the first time, found this shocking. Perhaps because of that examining magistrate, fresh from college, he was suddenly feeling an old man, a survival from the past.

All these girls smoking, and drinking whisky

and cocktails, were not for the men of his generation any more. A few of them, talking loudly, turned to stare at him curiously and rather brazenly.

He only had to bend forward and he could see the lighted fifth-floor windows up there, with a shadow passing across them now and then.

He had weighed the pros and cons. His first idea had been to wait for Jacques Sainval when he came out again. Fat, kindly Véronique Lachaume was in love, no doubt about that. Mightn't he cause her unhappiness? Wasn't there a danger of his causing a lovers' quarrel?

It was not the first time he'd been held back by scruples of that kind. But if his intuition was correct, wouldn't it be better for her to know how things stood?

He sipped his drink slowly, trying to imagine what was happening in the flat. Dinner must be ready. The two of them would be sitting down to it. He was giving them time to eat, and similarly time for Lapointe and the grocery woman to get under way.

'The same again . . .' he ordered.

Everything changes. It's like children growing up, you don't notice it while it's happening, only when it's happened.

His intimate enemy, as he liked to call him, the examining magistrate Coméliau, had retired now and become just an old gentleman taking his dog for its morning walk, arm-in-arm with a lady whose hair was dyed mauve.

Maigret had begun by finding around him, and later under his orders, inspectors who had never been on traffic duty, or taken their turn at the railway stations, but came from colleges. Nowadays he had some colleagues, with the same grade and salary as himself, who were scarcely forty years old. True, they all had law degrees, and many of them had two or three other university qualifications as well. Those chaps seldom left their offices, simply sending their subordinates out on investigations, and then sifting the results thus obtained.

In the course of his career he had seen police prerogatives being gradually whittled away, and now a new generation of examining magistrates was taking over. A team of young athletes was replacing the Coméliaus; like Angelot, they claimed the right to conduct an investigation from start to finish.

'How much is that?'

'Six hundred francs. . . .'

Prices were different too. He sighed, looked round for his coat, had to wait by the door till the cloakroom girl came.

'Thank you, Monsieur Maigret.'

Would the examining magistrate have been so punctilious in dealing with the Canon, for example, or some other professional thief, or with a navvy from the Quai de Javel?

Even though they were reduced to the almost disgusting poverty revealed on the Quai de la Gare, the Lachaumes were still patricians, a great *bourgeois* family whose name had been respected for over a century.

Would the younger generation still take that into account?

He was not actually asking himself questions, but he couldn't prevent his thoughts from revolving round various bothersome points. There are days when one is more than usually sensitive to certain aspects of the world. Yesterday had been All Souls' Day, the Feast of the Dead.

He shrugged his shoulders and crossed the street. Through their muslin curtains he saw the concierge and her husband sitting at a round table, gave them a slight wave as he went by, without being sure whether they had noticed him.

He took the lift to the fifth floor, rang the door bell, heard voices, followed by footsteps. It was fat Véronique who opened the door to him; her face was pinker than before, because she had just finished her hot soup, as he was soon to discover.

She was surprised to see him again, but did not seem worried.

'Did you forget something? Had you an umbrella?'

She glanced automatically towards the hat-stand in the passage.

'No. I'd just like a few words with your friend.'

'Ah!'

She closed the front door.

'Come in! This way. . . .'

She did not take him to the sitting-room, but to the kitchen. This was white-painted too, with chromium-plated electrical gadgets like those shown at Ideal Homes exhibitions. It was divided by a sort of balustrade, on one side of which a miniature dining-room had been fitted up. The steaming tureen was still on the table. Jacques Sainval had his spoon in his hand.

'It's Chief-Inspector Maigret, who'd like to talk to you. . . .'

The man got up, obviously ill at ease, hesitated whether to hold out his hand, finally did so.

'Delighted to meet you.'

'Please sit down. Go ahead with your dinner. . . .'

'I was just going to take away the soup.'

'Pay no attention to me.'

'You'd better give me your coat. It's very hot in here.'

She took his overcoat out to the hall. Maigret sat down, holding his unlighted pipe, with the feeling that Angelot, the magistrate, would have strongly disapproved of his behaviour.

'I only want to ask you one or two questions, Monsieur Sainval. I noticed your car down below. The red Panhard is yours, isn't it?'

'Yes.'

'Wasn't that car standing opposite the Pont National, yesterday evening, about six o'clock?'

Had Sainval been expecting this question? He showed no sign of alarm, appeared to be searching his memory.

'The Pont National?' he echoed.

'It's the last bridge before Ivry, a railway bridge. . . .'

Véronique, who had come back, was watching them both in surprise.

'I don't see. . . . No. . . . Wait a minute. . . . Yesterday afternoon. . . .'

'About six o'clock.'

'No. . . . Definitely not. . . .'

'You hadn't lent your car to anyone?'

It was not without reason that the chief-inspector offered him this loophole.

'I didn't exactly lend it, but one of my colleagues may possibly have used it. . . .'

'Do you generally park it in front of your office?'

'Yes.'

'With the key in it?'

'One has to take the risk, doesn't one? A bright-coloured car like that isn't very liable to be stolen, it would be too easy to trace.'

'Do you and your colleagues go to the office on Sundays?'

'We often do. . . .'

'Are you sure you're not lying, Jacquot?'

This was Véronique interrupting, as she put the joint on the table.

'Why should I be lying? You know perfectly well that the firm pays for the garage and the petrol. . . . If one of us has something urgent on hand and can't get hold of a car . . .'

'You don't know Paulette, of course?'

'Paulette who?'

Véronique Lachaume was not laughing now. In fact she had become extremely serious.

'My sister-in-law,' she explained.

'Ah, yes. . . . I vaguely remember your speaking about her. . . .'

'Do you know her?'

'By name.'

'And you know she lives on the Quai de la Gare?'

'Now you mention it. . . . Her address had slipped my memory. . . .'

Maigret had noticed a telephone in the concierge's lodge. There was one in Véronique's drawing-room as well.

'Might I make a telephone call?'

'You know where it is?'

He went to it by himself, rang down to the lodge.

'Maigret here. I'm on the fifth floor. . . . Yes. . . . Would you have a look out in the street to see whether a small black car has arrived? There should be a youngish man and an elderly woman sitting in it. . . . Ask them from me to be kind enough to come up here. . . .'

He had not lowered his voice. The pair in the kitchen had heard. It wasn't pleasant work, and he was trying to be as above-board as he could.

'I'm sorry, but I have to check up on something. . . .'

It looked to him as though Véronique's prominent eyes, so merry a little while ago, were moist. Her bosom had changed the rhythm of its rise and fall. She was forcing herself to eat, but her appetite had gone.

'You swear you're not hiding anything from me, Jacquot?'

Even the pet name 'Jacquot' was becoming embarrassing.

'I assure you, Nique . . .'

As Véronique had admitted, this was her first regular liaison, and despite her apparent cynicism it must mean a lot to her, this love. Did she already feel it threatened? Had she always had some doubt about the publicity agent's sincerity? Had she shut her eyes deliberately, because at the age of thirty-four she was tired of fooling around in a dinner-jacket and was yearning to get married like other women?

He was listening for the bell. When it rang he hurried into the passage and went to open the door.

As he had expected, the grocery woman had put on her Sunday best, with a black-fur-collared coat and an elaborate hat. Lapointe merely winked at his chief and said:

'I was as quick as I could manage.'

'Come in, Madame. It was you, I believe, who noticed a red car, yesterday evening, standing outside your premises?'

He was careful not to say 'shop'.

'Yes, Monsieur.'

'Come this way, please. . . .'

She stopped at the kitchen door in silence, turned to the chief-inspector and asked:

'What am I supposed to do?'

'Do you recognize anyone here?'

'Indeed I do.'

'Who?'

'The gentleman who's eating.'

Maigret went to the hat-stand for Sainval's hat and raincoat.

'I recognize those, too. Anyway, I'd already recognized the car out in the street. There's a dent in the right wing.'

Dry-eyed, with clenched teeth, Véronique Lachaume got up and put her plate into the sink. Her friend, too, stopped eating, sat hesitantly for a moment, then stood up, murmuring:

'All right!'

'What's all right?'

'I was there.'

'Thank you, Madame. You can drive her home now, Lapointe. Get her to sign a statement, just in case.'

When the three of them were alone again, Véronique said in a slightly hoarse voice:

'I wonder if you two would mind discussing your little affairs somewhere else than in my kitchen? . . . In the drawing-room, if you like. . . .'

Maigret realized that she wanted to be alone, perhaps to have a cry. He had spoilt her evening, and more than that, very likely. The little dinner for two had turned out badly.

'Come along. . . .'

He left the door open on purpose, for he felt

that as the daughter of the Lachaume family she had a right to hear what was said.

'Sit down, Monsieur Sainval.'

'May I smoke?'

'By all means.'

'Do you realize what you've just done?'

'What about you?'

Véronique's lover looked like a schoolboy caught in some prank; he had a sulky, shifty expression.

'I can tell you right away that you're mistaken.'

Maigret sat down facing him, filled his pipe. He said nothing, not wanting to make things easier for the other man. This, he realized, was a little unfair. Angelot, the magistrate, was not there. And Sainval wasn't insisting on his lawyer being present.

Some women doubtless found him handsome, but seen at close quarters, especially just now, he looked rather the worse for wear. Without the air of assurance that he usually assumed, one could feel he was weak, hesitant.

He would have been more at ease and at home in the American bar across the street.

'I've read the paper, like everyone else, and I can guess what you're thinking.'

'I'm not thinking anything, as yet.'

'Then why did you bring up that woman whom I don't know?'

'To make you admit that you were on the Quai de la Gare yesterday.'

'What does that prove?'

'Nothing, except that you know Paulette La-chaume.'

'And so what?'

He was regaining confidence; or rather, he was trying to put a bold face on things.

'I know hundreds of women, and I've never heard that that's a crime.'

'I am not accusing you of any crime, Monsieur Sainval.'

'Yet you come here, to my friend's flat, knowing quite well that . . . that . . .'

'That I'm putting you in an awkward position. For I imagine you've never told her about your goings-on with Paulette Lachaume?'

The man hung his head in silence. They could hear the rattle of plates and cutlery. To all appearances, Véronique was not listening.

'How long have you known her?'

Sainval was searching for an answer, still wondering whether or not to tell a lie. Whereupon Véronique broke in, showing that she had followed the conversation after all.

'It's my fault, Monsieur Maigret. Now I know. I've been nothing but an idiot, and I ought to have known where it would land me. . . .'

She had been crying in the kitchen, not much, but enough to make her eyes red. She was clutching a handkerchief, and her nostrils were still damp.

'Just now, when you came the first time, I gave you the answer to your question, without realizing it. You remember that about six weeks

128

or two months ago I thought I recognized my sister-in-law in the night-club? Jacques came to call for me that night, as he often does. I don't know why I mentioned it to him, because I'd never told him anything about my family.

'I don't remember exactly how it came up. I think I said:

' "My brother would have a nice surprise if he knew the kind of place his wife goes to! . . ."

'Something like that. . . . Jacques asked what my brother did, and it struck me as amusing to say:

' "Wafer biscuits!"

'We were very gay. We were walking arm-in-arm through the night.

' "Is he a pastrycook?"

' "Not exactly. Have you never heard of Lachaume's wafer-biscuits?"

'And as this meant nothing to him, I added:

' "His wife's worth at least two hundred million, perhaps more."

'Now do you understand?'

Though Maigret understood, he needed to know more.

'Did he question you about your sister-in-law?'

'Not then and there. That came later, one question at a time, casually, as it were. . . .'

'Were the two of you already thinking of getting married?'

'We'd been considering it, more or less seriously, for several weeks.'

'And you went on considering it?'

'I assumed it was settled, once and for all.'

Sainval muttered, in a voice he tried to make convincing:

'I've never changed my mind.'

'Then why did you get yourself acquainted with my sister-in-law?'

'Out of curiosity. . . . With no special purpose. . . . To begin with, she's married. . . . So . . .'

'So what?'

'It wasn't in my interest to . . .'

'Will you excuse me?' interrupted Maigret. 'I'd like to put a few more precise questions on my own. Tell me, Monsieur Sainval, where and when did you first meet Paulette Lachaume?'

'You want the exact date?'

'As near as you can manage.'

'It was on a Thursday, about four weeks ago, in a tea-room in the Rue Royale. . . .'

'So you go in for tea-rooms nowadays?' exclaimed Véronique with a burst of laughter.

She had no illusions left. She wasn't going to hang on. She knew it was all over and bore no grudge against her companion. It was only herself she was angry with.

'I don't suppose,' persisted Maigret, 'that you were there by pure chance. You had followed her. Probably since she left home. For how many days had you been watching her?'

'That was the second day.'

'In other words, hoping to make her acquaintance, you'd been on the watch in the afternoon, with your car, on the Quai de la Gare.'

He did not deny it.

'Paulette came out, probably in her blue Pontiac, and you followed her.'

'She left the car in the Place Vendôme and went shopping in the Rue Saint-Honoré.'

'In the tea-room you spoke to her?'

'Yes.'

'Did she seem surprised?'

'Very.'

'From which you inferred that she wasn't used to having men make up to her?'

It all hung together.

'When did you take her to your rooms?'

'I didn't take her home,' he protested.

'To an hotel?'

'No. A friend lent me his flat.'

Véronique interrupted again, sarcastically:

'You understand, Monsieur Maigret? The Rue de Ponthieu was quite good enough for me. But for a woman worth several hundred million francs he had to find somewhere more glamorous. Where was it, Jacques?'

'It belongs to an Englishman you don't know, on the Île Saint-Louis.'

'Did she often come to see you there?'

'Fairly often.'

'Every day?'

'Only just lately.'

'In the afternoon?'

'Sometimes in the evening too.'

'Yesterday?'

'Yes.'

'What happened yesterday evening?'

'Nothing in particular.'

'What did you talk about?'

Véronique again:

'Do you suppose they spent much time talking?'

'Answer me, Sainval.'

'Have you interrogated her?'

'Not yet.'

'You're going to?'

'Tomorrow morning, in the examining magistrate's office.'

'I didn't kill her brother-in-law. Anyhow, I had no reason to kill him.'

He fell silent for a moment, looking more thoughtful, added in a low voice:

'Neither had she.'

'Have you ever seen Léonard Lachaume?'

'Once when I was waiting on the quay, I saw him come out of the house.'

'Did he see you too?'

'No.'

'Where did you and Paulette have dinner yesterday?'

'In a restaurant in the Palais-Royal. You can verify that. We had a table on the *entresol*.'

'I know it!' broke in Véronique. 'It's called *Chez Marcel*. He's taken me there on the *entresol* too, the same table, I expect, in the left-hand corner. Am I right, Jacques?'

He made no reply.

'When you left the Quai de la Gare you didn't notice whether another car was following you?'

'No. It was raining. I didn't even look into the driving-mirror.'

'Afterwards you went to the flat on the Île Saint-Louis?'

'Yes.'

'You drove Paulette home?'

'No. She insisted on taking a taxi.'

'Why?'

'Because a red car is more noticeable at night, when the quay is deserted.'

'She was very much afraid of being seen with you?'

It was evident that Sainval didn't know what Maigret was getting at, or rather, that he was wondering what kind of a trap his questions concealed.

'I suppose so. It's fairly natural.'

'I take it, however, that she was on rather chilly terms with her husband?'

'There had been no intimate relations between them for years, and they had separate rooms. Armand's health is not good.'

'You were already calling him Armand?'

'There had to be some way of referring to him.'

'In fact, without ever having set foot in the Lachaumes' house, you regarded yourself in some sort as one of the family?'

Once again Véronique intervened, and this time she went straight to the point.

'Listen, both of you, there's no point in this cat-and-mouse game. You both know how things stand. So do I, I'm sorry to say, and I'm just a big fool.

'Although he's often at *Fouquet's*, *Maxim's*, and other smart places, Jacques has always been hard up, and his only possession is his car, assuming that's been paid for.

'I'd noticed already that he had bills chalked up in bars and restaurants. When he met me, he said to himself that a woman of my age, who's worked all her life, must have some money tucked away, and I was misguided enough to bring him here and tell him I'd just bought the flat.

'It's true. This place is my own. I'm even about to build myself a little house on the banks of the Marne.

'That sounded magnificent to him, and though I wasn't asking for anything of the kind, he began talking marriage.

'Only then I had the idiotic idea of telling him all about my sister-in-law and her millions. . . .'

'I have never taken money from women,' declared Sainval in a colourless voice.

'That's just what I'm saying. It wasn't worth while to get a small sum out of her now and then. Whereas by marrying her . . .'

'She's married. . . .'

'What's divorce for, then? Admit you've discussed it together.'

He hesitated, not knowing which way to turn. Hadn't Maigret told him he would be interrogating Paulette next day?

'I didn't take her seriously. I had put out a feeler, just from curiosity. . . .'

'So she was thinking of divorce. . . . And it

was so that the decree shouldn't go against her, that she was anxious not to be caught. . . . You see the idea, Monsieur Maigret? . . . I don't bear you any malice for bringing all this out. . . . It's not your fault. . . . You were looking for something else. . . . Sometimes when one's after big game one puts up a rabbit. . . .

'As for you, Jacquot, I'd be glad if you'd take away your dressing-gown and slippers and send me back my things. . . .

'It's almost time for me to go to work, and I must get into uniform. . . . The ladies are expecting me!'

A burst of slightly hysterical laughter shook her plump bosom.

'That'll teach me! . . . But you'd be making a mistake, Inspector, if you suspected Jacques of killing Léonard. . . . For one thing I don't see why he should have done it. . . . For another, between you and me, he's a phoney tough. . . . He'd have lost his nerve before he was over the wall. . . .

'Excuse me for not offering you a drink. . . .'

Her tears suddenly began to fall, without her being aware of it, and she didn't think to turn away her face. In a muffled voice, she commanded:

'Clear out, both of you. . . . It's high time I got dressed. . . .'

She pushed them into the passage, towards the hat-stand. Out on the landing, Sainval turned back:

'My dressing-gown and slippers . . . ?'

Instead of going to fetch them, she flung back at him:

'I'll send them to you all right. . . . Don't worry! No one else will use them. . . .'

The door closed behind them, and Maigret could have sworn he heard a sob, just one, followed by hurried footsteps.

Sainval and he waited in silence for the lift. As they stepped into it, the advertising agent murmured:

'Do you realize what you've done?'

'What about you?' retorted Maigret, lighting his pipe at last.

And that fool of a magistrate would have liked to be present right through the investigation! For the fun of it, no doubt?

7

He dreamt about it, like a schoolboy worrying over tomorrow's exam. And though Angelot, the magistrate, never put in an appearance, though Maigret never saw his face, his presence permeated the background all the same. It wasn't just one dream. It was a kind of string of dreams, separated by periods when the chief-inspector was half awake, sometimes even wide awake, during which he went on making the same effort.

It had begun rather pompously. He was informing the invisible magistrate:

'Very well, I'll show you my method. . . .'

To his mind this was a kind of rehearsal. He used the word 'method' ironically, of course, because for thirty years he'd been denying that he had any method. But never mind! He was not sorry to have things out with this insolently youthful magistrate.

Maigret was at the Quai de la Gare, all by himself in the dilapidated buildings, which had become so insubstantial that he could pass through the walls. But the interior was true to life, down to the least detail, including some the chief-inspector had forgotten in his waking moments.

'There you are! . . . Every evening, for years, they'd be sitting here . . .'

It was the drawing-room and Maigret was stoking the little stove, whose iron front showed a crack of brighter red, like a scar. He was arranging the characters in their places: the old couple, carved in wood; Léonard, whom he had to try to imagine alive and to whom he gave a thin, bitter smile; an impatient Paulette who kept jumping to her feet, thumbing through magazines, and was the first to announce that she was going to bed; and last of all Armand, who was tired and was taking some medicine.

'You understand, Monsieur Angelot, that is the capital point. . . .'

He didn't know what point.

'Every evening, for years. . . . Jean-Paul is already in bed. . . . The others, except Paulette, are all thinking the same thing. Léonard and his brother exchange glances from time to time. . . . Léonard will have to do the talking, because he's the eldest and because Armand doesn't dare. . . .'

Talking, in the dream, meant asking Zuber's daughter for money.

The firm of Lachaume was on the verge of

collapse; it was the oldest biscuit factory in Paris, an important institution, as valuable as one of those pictures of family groups that are put in museums, which have taken generations to create.

Somebody had a whole heap of money, dirty money, so dirty that old Zuber had been only too glad to give his daughter to a Lachaume so that she should have a respectable position in the world.

'You understand?'

For it was still in front of an invisible Angelot that he was working like this; an acrobat without a net. Difficult work. As when, in other dreams, he was raising himself through space by the strength of his hands.

He mustn't let the characters escape, melt into thin air.

'The old couple go away, followed by Armand, so as to leave the other two alone. It would be simpler if she would hand over a big sum at one go, but she stubbornly refuses to do that; perhaps her father, who was no fool, gave her that advice before he died. Only small amounts, for the end of the month. So that it has to be done over and over again. . . .'

The Lachaumes must have lied at the start, making out that given a few million francs the business would become prosperous once more, the house comfortable and cheerful, a setting for dinner-parties and receptions like any other big middle-class household. Paulette believed them, then ceased to do so.

The little talks with Léonard were repeated every month.

'How much?'

After which they would shut themselves up separately, each in one of those rooms. Each in one of those cells, to go on calculating. . . .

The corridor . . . the doors . . . The bathroom, at the far end, an ancient bathroom with a brown stain on the enamel, where the tap drips . . .

The Lachaumes are used to it . . . Perhaps in Zuber's household, in spite of the millions, they didn't use the bathroom? . . .

'All that, Monsieur Angelot, you have to assimilate . . .'

He repeated the word, stressing each syllable: '*As-si-mi-late!*'

. . . Léonard in his office downstairs, Armand in his, opposite the book-keeper, the biscuits being packed in the dispatch room, and an absurd trickle of smoke rising from the tall chimney, that imitation of a factory chimney . . .

Paulette in her car . . .

The day, the evening before. The grocery woman in her shop. It was Sunday, but the day before that was a public holiday, and the small local shopkeepers don't like to close for two days in succession. The red Panhard, towards six o'clock, with the so-called Sainval in his raincoat. Léonard following. In the blue Pontiac. The Palais-Royal. The restaurant . . .

It would have been interesting to superimpose

the different images, as in certain photographs, showing the Ivry police, the inspectors, Janvier, Lucas, all those who were questioning people, a barge at Corbeil, another on the Canal Saint-Martin, and Paul cutting up muscles and viscera, putting samples in test-tubes, the laboratory people measuring, analysing, looking through magnifying-glasses and microscopes . . .

Maigret smiled ironically.

'But what really matters . . .'

He refrained, out of modesty, from saying what really mattered, continuing to move from room to room, through the walls . . .

When Madame Maigret shook him awake, he was worn out, as if after a night in a train, and his neck was painful again.

'You talked several times during the night.'

'What did I say?'

'I couldn't understand. You mixed up the syllables . . .'

She didn't continue the subject. He had eaten without speaking to her, as though forgetting that he was at home and she was sitting opposite him.

Jacques Sainval had seemed surprised, the evening before, at being left free on the one condition that he didn't go out of Paris.

On reaching home, the chief-inspector had telephoned to Lapointe, who was on night-duty for the whole of this week, and had asked him to make certain investigations, to get a file together.

It was no longer raining, but the sky was no lighter, nor more cheerful-looking, and the people in the bus were crotchety.

Maigret had had himself roused earlier than usual, and when he arrived at the Quai des Orfèvres there was hardly anyone in the offices.

The first thing he saw, placed in full view, was the series of messages from the examining magistrate, who demanded that the chief-inspector should ring him up first thing in the morning, which, for a member of the Public Prosecutors staff, presumably meant nine o'clock.

This left him some time in hand, and he began by studying the statistics that Lapointe had left on his desk before going home to bed. He made no notes, merely memorizing some of the figures, not without a smile of satisfaction, for he had been pretty well right.

Next, he turned to the plan of the house at Ivry, prepared by the Judicial Identity branch.

With the plan went a bulky, meticulous report, for those fellows were not in the habit of overlooking the smallest detail. For instance, they had listed an old wheel off a child's bicycle, rusty and twisted, found in a corner of the courtyard.

Had it belonged to Jean-Paul's bicycle, or, very likely, to a bicycle once used by Armand, if not by Léonard? Or had some local resident got rid of it by throwing it over the wall instead of into the Seine?

The detail was suggestive, and there were a lot of others equally so, too many for them all to be kept in mind.

What he studied at greatest length was the inventory of the contents of Léonard's bedroom.

Eight white shirts, six of them very much worn, with darned collars and cuffs. . . . Six pairs of pants, patched. . . . Ten pairs of cotton socks and four pairs of woollen ones. . . . Five pairs of striped pyjamas. . . .

Everything was mentioned, the number of handkerchiefs, the condition of the comb, of the hairbrush and clothes-brush, with sketches showing the position of each item. As he had done in his dream during the night, Maigret strove to visualize the room and to place the various objects mentioned in the list.

. . . A black marble and bronze clock, no longer in working order. . . . Two three-branched marble and bronze candlesticks. . . . A wicker wastepaper basket containing a crumpled newspaper. . . . A 14-inch adjustable spanner, of the type used by plumbers. . . .

The bed was described with equal precision. One of the sheets, of fine linen and in excellent condition, was embroidered with the letter 'P', 1½ inches in height. . . .

Maigret held up two parted fingers, pictured the embroidered letter, sighed and, still reading, picked up the telephone.

'Get me Maître Radel. . . . The lawyer. . . . I don't know his number. . . .'

A few seconds later he was through to him.

'Hello? Maigret here. . . . I'd like you to ask your clients two questions, which will save my going to the Quai de la Gare and taking you along there. . . . Hello? Are you there?'

'Yes. I'm listening.'

The lawyer must be surprised at such punctilio from Maigret.

'The first question is about a spanner. . . . A fourteen-inch spanner. . . . It's in Léonard Lachaume's room, which is sealed up. . . . I'd like to know why it was there. . . . What? . . . Yes. . . . There may be some perfectly simple reason and I'd be glad to know it. . . .

'Another thing. . . . How many sheets are there in the house? . . . Yes, I'm sorry, I know it's a very down-to-earth subject. . . . Just a moment! . . . Ask whether all the sheets are embroidered with the letter "P", and if not, who were the embroidered ones used for. . . . How many sheets marked like that, and how many without a mark, or with a different one. . . . What? . . . Yes, that's all. . . . At least. . . . I expect you'll take refuge in professional secrecy. . . . How long have you been the Lachaumes' lawyer? . . .'

There was no answer from the other end. Maître Radel was hesitating. Maigret had been surprised, the day before, to find such a young, practically unknown lawyer in a house where he would have expected to meet a crafty old pettifogger.

'What did you say? . . . A week? . . . And lastly, might I ask for whom, precisely, you are acting? . . . Somebody sent for you a week ago, or called on you. . . .'

He listened, shrugged his shoulders, and finally, when the voice stopped speaking, rang off. As he had expected, Radel refused to answer that last question.

He was reaching out for one of his pipes when the telephone rang. It was Angelot, the magistrate, already in his office well before nine o'clock.

'Chief-Inspector Maigret?'

'Yes, Monsieur Angelot.'

'You had my messages?'

'Certainly. I have read them carefully.'

'I should like to see you as soon as possible.'

'I know. I'm just waiting for one telephone call, in a few minutes, I hope, before coming round to your office.'

Whereupon he did wait, without doing anything else, except smoke and stand looking out of the window. It took six minutes. Radel had been quick.

'I asked first about the spanner. . . . Old Catherine remembers that very well. . . . About a fortnight ago, Léonard Lachaume was indisposed by a smell of gas in his room. . . . They don't use gas any more except in the kitchen, but in the old days the bedrooms were lit by gas and the system is still there. All that was done was to block the pipes with bolts. So Léonard fetched a spanner from the ground-floor workshop. . . . He forgot to take it back, and it's been in a corner of his room ever since. . . .'

'What about the sheets?'

'I couldn't get an exact list, because there are some at the laundry. . . . There are several different marks. . . . The oldest, which are very worn, bear the initials "N.F." and date from the time when the old couple were married. . . . In those days a bride brought with her enough sheets to last a lifetime. . . . They're made of thick cambric and there are several pairs left. . . . Then there are sheets marked "M.L.", that belonged to Léonard's late wife. . . . Twelve pairs, I'm told. . . . Including one scorched by an overheated iron. . . . Six pairs of almost new sheets, cotton, without initials. . . . Lastly, two dozen better-quality sheets coming from Paulette Lachaume. . . .'

'Are they marked with a "P"?'

'Yes.'

'I suppose the idea was that only she used those?'

'I didn't venture to press that point. I was just told those were her own sheets.'

'Thank you.'

'Might I ask you . . .'

'Nothing, Maître. . . . I know nothing as yet. . . . Excuse me. . . .'

Taking no file with him, he opened the door of the inspectors' office, where Lucas had just arrived.

'If anyone asks for me, I'm with the examining magistrate.'

He had a key to the glass-panelled door leading from Police Headquarters into the *Palais de Justice*, which has been kept carefully locked ever since a prisoner made a getaway through it.

As usual, he recognized several old acquain-

tances sitting on the benches, some of them between two policemen. He also saw the Canon,
who was waiting by the door of one of the examining magistrates and who, without a word,
indicated the handcuffs that had been clamped
on him, shrugging his shoulders as though to
say:

'That's what they're like on this side of the
door!'

It was indeed a different world, with a dull
smell of bureaucracy and red tape.

He knocked on Angelot's door, found him
seated at his desk, smooth-shaven, surrounded
by a faint smell of lavender. His secretary, at the
end of the table, was hardly older than he.

'Sit down, Chief-Inspector. I was rather surprised, yesterday, to have no news from you
right through the afternoon and evening. Am
I to conclude that you have discovered nothing, that you have taken no steps likely to interest me?'

The secretary was still there, holding a pencil
as though ready to make notes, but fortunately
he was not making any.

'Have you been back to the Quai de la Gare?'

'I myself, no.'

'So you have not seen any members of the
family or staff again?'

'No.'

'I take it that you and your subordinates have
been attending to the case, all the same? I've
been thinking about it at great deal myself; and

147

I must admit that although the sum stolen was so trifling, I keep coming back to the idea of a burglary. . . .'

Maigret said nothing, reflecting on the difference between his dream and reality. Was it truly worth while explaining, trying to get the magistrate to understand what . . .

He waited for definite questions.

'What do you think about it?' he was asked at last.

'About a burglary?'

'Yes.'

'I had some figures looked up for you. Do you know how many burglaries there have been in Paris in the last ten years at night in private houses or flats, while the occupants were at home?'

The magistrate looked at him, surprised, intrigued.

'Thirty-two,' went on Maigret off-handedly. 'Just over three per year. Apart from the fact that more than a dozen of them must be credited to a kind of artist or lunatic whom we arrested three years ago and who's still in prison, a young chap of twenty-five, who lived with his sister, had no mistress and no men friends, and whose one passion was to bring off the most difficult feats, such as going into a bedroom where a married couple lay asleep and taking the jewellery without giving the alarm. He was never armed, of course.'

'Why do you say "of course"?'

'Because the professional burglar never is

armed. He knows the law, from experience, and keeps his risks down to the minimum.'

'But nearly every week . . .'

'Yes, nearly every week you see in the papers that an old tradeswoman, a haberdasher, or the keepers of some back-street or suburban shop have been done in. . . . But those aren't really burglaries. . . . Crimes like that are committed by young thugs who are simple-minded, often even half-witted. . . . I also wanted to find out how many real burglaries, in the last ten years, were accompanied or followed by murder. . . . Three, Monsieur. . . . One burglar used a monkey-wrench he had in his pocket. . . . The second picked up a poker on the spot, which he used when he was taken by surprise and threatened. . . . The third did have a firearm, a Luger he'd brought back from the war. . . .'

He repeated:

'Only one! . . . And that was not a 6.35 automatic. . . . I don't think you'd find in the whole of Paris a single professional burglar or criminal using one of those weapons; they are what honest citizens keep in the drawer of the bedside table, and jealous women carry in their handbags. . . .'

'If I understand correctly, you rule out the hypothesis of a burglary?'

'I do.'

'Even by an employee, or former employee, for instance?'

'During the evening a Belgian bargeman, whom my men managed to trace, saw somebody

149

propped on a ladder inside the yard, smashing the broken glass on top of the wall.'

'During the evening, or after two o'clock in the morning?'

'During the evening, about ten o'clock.'

'In other words, four hours before the crime?'

'Four hours before the crime.'

'If that is correct, what do you infer from it?'

'Nothing so far. You asked me to keep you informed.'

'Have you made any other discoveries?'

'Paulette Lachaume has a lover.'

'She told you so? I thought you . . .'

'I haven't seen her. She has told me nothing. It was her sister-in-law who unintentionally put me on the track. . .'

'What sister-in-law?'

'Véronique Lachaume.'

'Where did you find her?'

'In her flat, in the Rue François Ier. She works as hostess in a nightclub of a rather specialized type, the *Amazone*, in the Rue Marbeuf. Her lover, whom she was expecting to marry in the near future, is also Paulette's lover. . . .'

'Did he admit it?'

'Yes.'

'What sort of man is he?'

'The kind you see a great many of round about the Champs-Elysées. . . . His job is advertising. . . . Owes money in all the bars. . . . To begin with, he thought he'd marry Véronique, who owns her flat and has some savings. . . . When he heard about the sister-in-law and her

150

millions, he arranged things so as to meet her, became her lover, and the day before yesterday he had dinner with her and then took her to a flat on the Île Saint-Louis which is lent to him on occasion by an English friend. . . .'

Purposely, not without a mischievous satisfaction, he was pouring out this mixture of information which the magistrate was struggling to classify in his mind.

'You kept him at the Quai des Orfèvres?'

'I didn't take him there.'

'Where does that get us?'

'I don't know. If we dismiss the hypothesis of a burglar or a lunatic and if we credit what the bargeman said, we are driven to the conclusion that the crime was committed by a member of the household. Now, the Judicial Identity men have found a fourteen-inch spanner in Léonard Lachaume's room.'

'The murderer used a revolver. . . .'

'I know. That spanner weighs over two pounds. According to Catherine, the servant, it had been in Léonard's room for the last fortnight, since he had used it to tighten a bolt stopping up the gas pipe. . . .'

'What other information have you?'

The magistrate was becoming irritated by Maigret's ironical placidity. It was obvious, even to the secretary, who was gazing down at the table in embarrassment, that the chief-inspector had deliberately adopted an attitude which, though not hostile nor definitely truculent, was hardly friendly.

151

'One can't really call it information. . . . For instance, I've just obtained a list of the sheets used in the house. . . .'

'The sheets?'

'Only one sheet, in Léonard's room, is blood-stained. . . . But it is embroidered with a "P" and belongs to Paulette. . . .'

'Is that all?'

'The day before yesterday she left the house on foot, in the rain, at about six o'clock, to meet her lover, who was waiting for her, in a red car, a little way along the quay in front of a grocery. At about the same time, Léonard Lachaume went out, driving his sister-in-law's car, a blue Pontiac. . . . The couple went to a quiet restaurant in the Palais-Royal. *Chez Marcel*. . . . Léonard is said to have arrived home at nine o'clock. . . . An hour later, someone, from inside the yard, was crushing the broken glass along the top of the wall with some heavy object, probably a hammer. . . .

'Paulette, after a visit to the Englishman's flat, on the Quai de Bourbon, went home by taxi. . . .'

'Why not in her lover's car?'

'Because at night she was afraid of being noticed.'

'She told you that?'

'Her lover told me. In the corridor she exchanged greetings with Léonard, who was in his dressing-gown. . . .'

Maigret's features suddenly froze, and for a moment he seemed abstracted.

'What are you thinking about?'

'I don't know yet I shall have to check up. . . .'

All this was very different from his dream, when he had given such a brilliant demonstration of his methods to the invisible examining magistrate. And they were not at the Quai de la Gare. The atmosphere of the house was lacking, the things in it, the past and the present, the visible and the invisible.

All the same he was playing a part, consciously. With poor Coméliau, who had for so long been his personal enemy, there had been open hostility, the old, unacknowledged but always latent rivalry between the Public Prosecutor's Office and the Quai des Orfèvres.

Other magistrates preferred to let him have his own way and wait patiently for him to bring them a complete file, preferably including a signed confession.

In dealing with the new magistrate, Angelot, he was swaggering, in spite of himself, playing, so to speak, the character of Maigret as some people imagined him.

He was a bit ashamed of himself, but he couldn't help it. This was a meeting of two generations, and he wasn't sorry to show this greenhorn . . .

'In conclusion . . . ?'

'I have come to no conclusion, *Monsieur le Juge*.'

'If, as you seem to say, it was a member of the family . . .'

'Of the family or the household.'

'Meaning you include the old hunchbacked servant among the suspects?'

'I don't rule out anyone. I'm not going to quote you any more statistics. Three months ago a man killed his neighbour, with a 6.35 automatic, by the way, because the neighbour persisted in playing his wireless at full volume.'

'I don't see the connexion.'

'At first sight it was an idiotic, inexplicable crime. But the murderer is a completely disabled ex-serviceman, who's been trepanned twice and spends his days in pain in an arm-chair. He has nothing but his pension to live on. The neighbour was a tailor, of foreign extraction, who worked at home; he'd been in trouble after the Liberation, and had got out of it. . . .'

'I still don't see . . .'

'What I'm getting at is this. . . . What at first sight appears to be a ridiculous motive—a little music more or less—becomes for the disabled man, when you come to think it over, a vital question. . . . In other words, in the circumstances, the crime was explicable, almost inevitable.'

'I can't see any similar situation at the Quai de la Gare.'

'Yet there must be something, *at least in the mind of the person who killed Léonard Lachaume.* Except for certain rather rare pathological cases, people don't kill except for definite, imperative motives.'

'Have you found that motive in the case we are considering?'

'I've found several.'

But the chief-inspector was suddenly tired of the role he had been drawn into playing.

'I must apologize . . .' he murmured.

He was sincere about it.

'What for?'

'For everything. Never mind. just now, while talking to you, I had an idea. If you will allow me to make a telephone call, we shall perhaps find things growing clearer.'

The magistrate pushed the telephone towards him.

'Get me the Judicial Identity branch, please. . . . Hello? . . . Yes. . . . Hello? . . . Who's speaking? . . . That you, Moers? Maigret here. . . . I had the report. . . . Yes. . . . It isn't about that I want to talk to you, it's about the inventory. . . . It's quite complete, I suppose? . . . What? . . . I know. . . . I'm quite sure it was done very thoroughly. . . . I just want to be certain that nothing can have been left out. . . .

'. . . The man who typed it may have skipped a line? . . . You have the original list by you? . . . If you'll take it. . . . Good. . . . Now, see if there's no mention of a dressing-gown. . . . I ran over the list rather hurriedly in my office, and it might have escaped me. . . . A dressing-gown, yes. . . . A man's, that's it. . . . I'll hold on. . . .'

He listened while Moers read the list in an undertone.

'No. There's no mention of a dressing-gown. Anyhow, I was there and I didn't see one. . . .'

'Thanks, old man.'

The magistrate and he looked at each other in silence. At last Maigret murmured, as though he were unsure of himself:

'Perhaps, at the stage we've reached, an interrogation might produce some results!'

'An interrogation of whom?'

'That's what I'm wondering.'

And not merely because he was seeking what he sometimes called the point of least resistance. Today there was a personal question as well.

He felt sure Judge Angelot would insist on the interrogation taking place in his office. Perhaps he might even want to conduct it himself?

Maigret felt uncomfortable at the thought of summoning old Lachaume, who already resembled one of the ancestral portraits hanging in the ground-floor office. He would have to be separated from his wife, who could hardly be brought along too. It wasn't even certain that old Lachaume still had all his wits. His eyes seemed to be gazing inwards, and Maigret suspected that he was living entirely among his memories.

As for Catherine, she'd be aggressive, for she was a woman of one idea and would not depart from it. She would deny everything in the teeth of the evidence, not giving a fig for logic. He'd have to look at her hunchbacked figure, listen to her shrill voice.

He didn't know Jean-Paul, had never had a chance to set eyes on him, since the boy had been hurriedly whisked away to boarding-school.

The kid might accidentally have provided some valuable information, but the chief-inspector could imagine how much the examining magistrate would shrink from the idea of bothering a child whose father had died two nights before.

There remained Armand and Paulette.

Armand's epileptic fits were an argument against choosing him. With his back to the wall, might he not be tempted to indulge in one, whether real or sham?

'I think Paulette Lachaume would be the best person to interrogate,' he finally decided, heaving a sigh.

'Have you any specific questions to ask her?'

'Some. Others will develop out of her replies.'

'Do you want me to inform her lawyer?'

Radel would be there, of course. With Angelot, everything would be done according to the rules. It was not without regret that Maigret relinquished his own office, his habits, his little ways, such as choosing the moment to have sandwiches and beer or coffee sent up, or having himself relieved by one of his inspectors, who would innocently begin the interrogation all over again.

The day would come before long when all that would be over and done with, and Maigret's work would be carried out by fellows like Angelot, gentlemanly chaps with a sheaf of degrees.

'I rang him up this morning,' the chief-inspector confessed.

The magistrate frowned.

'About this interrogation?'

He was already prompt to insist on his rights.

'No. To ask him for two of the pieces of information I've just given you. To avoid disturbing the Lachaume family, I decided to apply for it through him.'

'Hello? . . . Get me Maître Radel's office, please. André Radel, that's it. . . . Hello? . . . André? . . .'

The day before, at the Quai de la Gare, Maigret had not heard the two men calling one another by their Christian names.

'Listen. . . . I have Chief-Inspector Maigret in my office. . . . The investigation has reached a point at which certain interrogations seem to be necessary. . . . Yes, of course, in my office. . . . No! I don't intend to disturb the old parents. . . . Nor him . . . for the moment, at any rate. . . . What? . . . What does the doctor say? Oh! . . . Paulette Lachaume, yes. . . . This morning, for choice. . . . Very well. . . . I'll wait for you to call me. . . .'

He rang off, thought fit to explain:

'We went through law school together. . . . He tells me Armand Lachaume is in bed. . . . He had a rather serious attack yesterday evening. . . . The doctor was sent for and is at his bedside again this morning. . . .'

'And Paulette?'

'Radel's going to ring me back. He hopes to bring her along here later in the morning.'

The magistrate seemed embarrassed, cleared his throat, fidgeted with his paper-knife.

'It would be more in order, at the present stage, for me to put the questions, while you intervene only if it becomes necessary. . . . I take it you see no objection to that?'

Maigret saw a great many objections, but what would be the use of saying so?

'Just as you wish.'

'On the other hand it is only natural, I think, for you to give me in writing, before she arrives, the points on which you think I should lay emphasis.'

Maigret nodded.

'Just a few words on a piece of paper. Quite unofficially.'

'Of course.'

'Have you any information about Léonard Lachaume's late wife?'

'She served the same function as Zuber's daughter.'

'That being?'

'To keep the house on the quay and the biscuit factory alive, if one can call it alive, for a time. A similar background, too. Her father began as a foreman and made a fortune as a government contractor. Her dowry was used to stop the leaks.'

'And the money she left?'

'She didn't leave anything, because her father is still alive and may last a long time.'

First Léonard. Then Armand.

Wasn't there something rather touching about this determination to keep the firm afloat, when by all the laws of the business world it should have foundered long ago?

Was it not something like the behaviour of the disabled ex-serviceman who had shot his neighbour because he tortured him from morning to night by turning his radio full on?

It was no accident that Maigret had referred to that case. True, he had been acting a part before the examining magistrate, but in essentials he had been honest with himself.

'Hello, yes. . . . What did she say? . . . How long do you think that will take? . . . About half past eleven? . . . Right. . . . Oh no! It'll be in my office. . . .'

Was Radel so afraid of the interrogation taking place in Maigret's office? Angelot had reassured him, as though saying:

'In my office it will all be done in the proper way. . . .'

The chief-inspector sighed and stood up:

'I'll be here a little before half past eleven.'

'Don't forget to note down the questions that . . .'

'I'll think about them.'

The poor Canon was still waiting resignedly on his bench, between two policemen, for 'his' magistrate to deign to receive him. Maigret winked at him as he went by, and when he got back to his own office, banged the door savagely behind him.

8

WITH his elbows resting heavily on his desk,
his forehead supported on his left hand, he wrote
a few words, between short puffs of his pipe,
then sat for quite a time staring at the watery-
looking rectangle of the window.

As though on the eve of an examination, in
the days when he had been for two years a med-
ical student, he had re-read all the reports, including, three times over, the famous inventory,
of which he was becoming heartily sick.

But he felt less like a student than like a boxer
who, within an hour, perhaps within a few minutes, would be staking his reputation, his very
career, calling forth jeers or an ovation.

The comparison was not accurate, of course.
The magistrate, Angelot, could not influence a
career which in any case would soon end in
retirement. And the journalists would know

nothing of what was about to take place within the four walls of an office in the *Palais de Justice*.

So there was no question of an ovation. The worst that could happen to Maigret was a reprimand, and, in future, ironical or pitying glances from certain young magistrates to whom Angelot would undoubtedly relate the story.

'As for Maigret and his hunches, have you ever heard . . .'

As soon as he got back to his office, he had called Lucas to give him instructions, and all the inspectors available were now on footwork, as it is called, in the neighbourhood of the Palais-Royal this time, questioning shopkeepers, news-vendors, visiting in their homes or offices any customers of *Chez Marcel* who had been dining on the ground floor on Sunday evening and might have seen something through the windows.

There was only a tiny detail involved, but at the last moment it might become important, even prove conclusive.

Maigret had written out his questions once, then, thinking his writing was not legible enough, had re-copied them.

At ten minutes past eleven, after some hesitation, he had put the sheet of paper into an envelope and sent it by hand to the *Palais de Justice*.

This was a sporting gesture on his part. He was giving Judge Angelot time to get ready, and, in so doing, revealing his own cards.

He did this not so much out of generosity, however, as by the wish to arrive at the last moment and thus avoid another conversation with the magistrate before the interrogation began.

'If anyone rings me up, I'm not in, unless it's one of our chaps.'

He would not speak to Angelot before Paulette appeared, not even on the telephone. Now he was roaming round his office, pausing a moment to look out at the cruel grey Seine, at the black ants going to and fro across the Pont Saint-Michel and weaving their way among the buses.

From time to time he shut his eyes, the better to envisage the house on the Quai de la Gare, and occasionally he uttered a few words under his breath.

Eleven-twenty . . . twenty-three . . . twenty-five. . . .

'I'll be off now, Lucas. If anything fresh comes in, tell them to let me know, and to insist on speaking to me personally.'

As the chief-inspector's bulky figure moved away along the corridor, Lucas's lips outlined, as it were, an inaudible word which began with an 's'.

Maigret caught sight of Maître Radel in the distance, steering Paulette Lachaume towards the magistrate's office; she was wearing a beaver coat, and a hat of the same fur, and the three of them went in almost together, which made the magistrate raise his eyebrows. Did he imagine Maigret had stolen a march on him by waylaying the young woman and her lawyer?

Radel unconsciously reassured him:

'Hullo! Were you just behind us?'

'I came by the side door.'

The magistrate had risen, though he did not actually advance to meet his visitor.

'I must apologize, Madame, for bringing you here. . . .'

She was tired, that could be seen in her face, which looked blurred, almost ravaged. Glancing round mechanically for a chair, she murmured:

'I understand. . . .'

'Please sit down. You too, Maître Radel. . . .'

The two men were not using each other's Christian names now, and to all appearances their relations had never been on anything but a strictly professional footing.

'I believe, Madame, that you already know Chief-Inspector Maigret. . . .'

'Yes, we met at the Quai de la Gare. . . .'

He waited for Maigret to sit down in his turn, near the door, a little behind the others. The seating arrangements took some time. At last the magistrate sat down, looked to see that his secretary was ready to take down the conversation in shorthand, then cleared his throat.

It was his turn to feel awkward, for this time the roles were reversed: he was in the centre of the stage, while Maigret had become the spectator, the onlooker.

'Maître Radel, some of my questions may seem curious to you, as well as to your client. . . . But I think she owes it to herself to answer them frankly, even those that concern her private life. . . .'

164

She had been expecting this; Maigret felt sure of it, just by looking at her. So she wouldn't be taken by surprise. Radel must have warned her that the police had certainly got wind of her liaison with Sainval.

'The first question concerns you, too, Maître, but I particularly wish the reply to come from Madame Lachaume. . . . On what date, Madame, did you feel the need to consult a barrister? . . .'

Radel was about to protest. A glance from his fellow-lawyer gave him pause, and he turned to his client, who had herself turned towards him, murmuring timidly:

'Must I answer?'

'It will be better if you do.'

'Three weeks ago.'

Looking at the desk, where the judge, on purpose, had laid out various documents, including copies of the reports and the inventory, Maigret noticed that Angelot was not using his little sheet of paper, but that the questions had been copied on another sheet.

From now on, Angelot regularly glanced at his secretary whenever he was about to speak, to make sure that he was allowing time for everything to be taken down.

The atmosphere was still impersonal, official, and there was no sense of emotion in the air as yet.

'When your father died, it was his usual notary, Maître Wurmster, who dealt with the estate, was it not? And he had the assistance of a barrister who had also acted for your father, Maître Tobias?'

She nodded, but he insisted on an audible reply.

'Yes.'

'Had you a particular reason, three weeks ago, not to turn to your father's lawyer, that is, to Maître Tobias, but to another member of the Bar?'

Radel intervened.

'I do not see the connexion between that question and the events at the Quai de la Gare.'

'You will see it presently, Maître. I would ask your client to be good enough to reply.'

And Paulette Lachaume, almost inaudibly:

'Yes, I think so.'

'You mean you had a reason for changing your lawyer?'

'Yes.'

'Wasn't it that you wished for the help of a specialist?'

Radel was about to protest again, when the magistrate forestalled him.

'By specialist, I mean a lawyer well known for his success in a particular field. . . .'

'Perhaps.'

'And was it not, in fact, about the prospect of a divorce that you went to consult Maître Radel?'

'Yes.'

'Did your husband know of this at the time?'

'I had said nothing to him about it.'

'Might he have suspected your intentions?'

'I don't think so.'

'And your brother-in-law?'

'I don't think so either. Not at that time.'

'Did you pay out money to meet the expenses at the end of last month?'

'Yes.'

'You signed the cheque without arguing about the amount?'

'Yes. I hoped it would be the last. I didn't want a scene.'

'The plans for the divorce were ready?'

'Yes.'

'When was it that someone in the house on the Quai de la Gare got wind of your intentions?'

'I don't know.'

'But the suspicion did exist, during these last few days at any rate ?'

'I believe so.'

'What makes you believe so?'

'A letter from Maître Radel never reached me.'

'How long ago should that letter have reached you?'

'A week ago.'

'Who used to open the mail?'

'My brother-in-law.'

'So that in all probability Léonard Lachaume intercepted the letter from Maître Radel. Did you have the impression that from then onwards there was something different about the Lachaumes' attitude towards you?'

She visibly hesitated.

'I'm not sure.'

'You did have that impression?'

'My husband seemed to be avoiding me. One evening, when I got home . . .'

'When was that?'

'Last Friday.'

'Go on. You were saying that last Friday, when you got home . . . What time was it?'

'Seven o'clock. . . . I'd been shopping in town. . . . I found everybody in the drawing-room. . . .'

'Old Catherine too?'

'No.'

'So there were your father- and mother-in-law, Léonard and your husband. Was Jean-Paul there?'

'I didn't see him. I suppose he was in his own room.'

'What happened when you arrived?'

'Nothing. Usually I got back later. They weren't expecting me and they all stopped talking. It seemed to me that they were all embarrassed. That evening my mother-in-law didn't dine with us, but went straight up to her room. . . .'

'Until recently, if I'm not mistaken, Jean-Paul slept on the first floor, in the room next to his father's, the room that had formerly been his mother's. . . . When did he move up to the second floor, where he is now alone with the three old people?'

'A week ago.'

'Was it the boy himself who proposed the change?'

'No. He didn't like it.'

'It was your brother-in-law's idea?'

'He wanted to turn Jean-Paul's room into a private study, where he could go after dinner.'

'Was he in the habit of working in the evening?'

'No.'

'What was your reaction?'

'I felt worried.'

'Why?'

She looked at her lawyer. The latter uneasily lit a cigarette. Maigret, motionless in his corner, would have liked to light his pipe, which lay, ready filled, in his pocket, but he didn't dare.

'I don't know. I was frightened. . . .'

'Frightened of what?'

'Of nothing definite. . . . I'd have preferred to get things over without a row, without arguments, tears, pleading. . . .'

'You mean your divorce?'

'Yes. For them, I knew it was a catastrophe. . . .'

'Because since your marriage it is you who have kept the place going. Is that not so?'

'Yes. In any case I meant to leave a certain sum for my husband. I'd spoken to Maître Radel about it. But I wanted to be out of the house the day Armand was served with the papers. . . .'

'Jacques Sainval knew about all this?'

On hearing the name she blinked, and then murmured, with no further sign of surprise:

'Of course. . . .'

The magistrate sat in silence for a little while, looking down at his notes. Before resuming, not without a touch of solemnity, he could not resist a glance at Maigret.

'In fact, Madame Lachaume, your departure meant final collapse for the biscuit factory and for the family as well.'

'I've already told you I would have left money for them.'

'Enough to manage for a long time?'

'For a year at any rate.'

Maigret remembered the words engraved on the brass plate, *Established in 1817*.

Nearly a century and a half. What was one year in comparison? For a century and a half the Lachaumes had held out, and all of a sudden, because a chit like Paulette had made the acquaintance of a greedy advertising agent . . .

'Have you made a will?'

'No.'

'Why not?'

'In the first place, because I have no children. In the second place, because I intended to marry again as soon as it was legally possible.'

'According to your marriage settlement, the fortune goes to the surviving partner of the marriage?'

'Yes.'

'How long have you been frightened?'

Radel tried to put her on her guard, but too late, for she was already answering, without realizing the danger:

'I don't know. . . . A few days. . . .'

'Frightened of what?'

This time she did react, and they saw her fingers clench, her face take on an expression of terror.

'I don't see what you're getting at. Why are you questioning me and not *them*?'

Maigret thought fit to glance encouragingly at the hesitant magistrate.

'Your decision to divorce was final?'

'Yes.'

'Nothing the Lachaumes might have said would have induced you to stay?'

'No. I'd sacrificed myself for long enough. . . .'

For once the words, so often pronounced by women, were not exaggerated. For how long, once she was married, could she have preserved any illusion as to the part she played in the patrician house on the Quai de la Gare?

She had not rebelled. She had done her best to refloat the firm, at least to stop up the holes, and prevent it from foundering once and for all.

'Did you love your husband?'

'I thought so, right at the beginning.'

'You never had any sexual relations with your brother-in-law?'

The magistrate brought out this question with visible distaste, and resented Maigret's having obliged him to ask it.

As she hesitated, he added:

'Did he never try?'

'Once, a long time ago. . . .'

'A year, two years, three years after your marriage?'

'About a year after, when Armand and I moved into separate rooms.'

'You rejected Léonard's advances?'

'Yes.'

The silence that followed was graver, more oppressive than on previous occasions. The atmosphere had imperceptibly changed, and there was a feeling that from now on every word would carry weight, that they were moving towards some redoubtable truth not yet mentioned by anyone.

'Who used to use the sheets embroidered with your initial?'

She answered too quickly. Radel hadn't time to warn her of the trap.

'I did, of course.'

'And no one else?'

'I don't think so. Possibly my husband, occasionally.'

'Not your brother-in-law?'

As she remained silent, he repeated:

'Not your brother-in-law?'

'Not in the ordinary way.'

'There were enough other sheets in the house for all the family's beds?'

'I suppose so.'

'Did you tell Jacques Sainval you were afraid?'

She was beginning to give ground, not knowing which way to look, her hands so tightly clenched that the knuckles were turning white.

'He wanted me to leave the Quai de la Gare at once. . . .'

'Why did you not do so?'

'I was waiting for the divorce papers to be ready. It was only a matter of two or three days longer. . . .'

'In other words, if it were not for your brother-in-law's death, you would have left the house today or tomorrow?'

She sighed.

'Did it occur to you, last week that someone might try to stop you from going?'

She turned to her lawyer.

'Give me a cigarette. . . .'

And Angelot continued:

'. . . to stop you by no matter what means?'

'I don't know now. You're confusing me.'

She lit the cigarette, put the lighter back into her bag.

'Didn't Sainval warn you to be careful, especially after noticing that your brother-in-law was following you?'

She raised her head sharply.

'How do you know that?'

'When did he follow you?'

'The day before yesterday.'

'Not before that?'

'I'm not sure. . . . Last Thursday, I thought I caught sight of him on the Quai de Bourbon. . . .'

'You were in Sainval's friend's flat?'

She looked at Maigret reproachfully, as though she knew it was he who was responsible for these discoveries.

'Léonard had taken your car?'

'I allowed him to. . . .'

'And you saw him out of the window as he went past?'

'He was driving slowly and looking up at the house. . . .'

'It was then that Sainval gave you a revolver?'

'*Monsieur le Juge* . . .'

Radel raised his hand, stood up.

'At the point we have now reached, I ask your permission to have a short talk with my client.'

The judge and Maigret exchanged glances. Maigret batted his eyelids.

'On condition that it is really short. You may use this room.'

He signed to his secretary. The three men went out into the corridor where Maigret, without loss of time, lit his pipe. He and the magistrate walked up and down among the general concourse, while the secretary sat on the bench beside the door.

'Do you still consider, Monsieur Maigret, that it is not possible to obtain the same results, quietly, without shouting, without theatrical effects, in an examining magistrate's office as at the Quai des Orfèvres?'

What would be the use of replying that all he had done was to reel off the questions prepared by the chief-inspector?

'If things happened as I am beginning to believe they did, Radel will advise her to speak up. . . . It's in her own interest. . . . He should have insisted on it from the first. . . . Unless she hadn't even told the truth to him. . . . Suppose

174

she hadn't replied to my questions, or had been a good liar. Where should we be now?'

Maigret nudged his arm, for he had just caught sight of a faltering figure, a good way off along the endless corridor.

It was Armand Lachaume, obviously lost in the maze of the *Palais de Justice*, reading the notices outside the doors.

'You saw him? We'd better go in again before . . .'

Lachaume had not caught sight of them as yet, and the magistrate knocked at the door of his own office and went in, followed by the chief-inspector and the secretary.

'I apologize. Unforeseen circumstances oblige me to . . .'

Paulette Lachaume, whom they had caught standing up, sat down again, paler than before but more composed, as though relieved. Radel seemed about to make a speech. Just as he opened his mouth the telephone rang, the magistrate picked up the receiver, listened, held it out to the chief-inspector.

'It's for you.'

'Maigret here, yes . . . Two people saw the car? . . . Good! . . . The description fits? . . . Thank you. No . . . See you later. . . .'

He rang off and announced in an expressionless voice:

'Léonard Lachaume was outside the restaurant in the Palais-Royal the night before last.'

Maître Radel gave a shrug, as though all that business was over and done with now. But if the interrogation had taken a different turn, the information would have been valuable, nevertheless.

'My client, *Monsieur le Juge*, is prepared to tell the whole truth, and as you will see, it puts others in a worse light than herself. You must understand, too, and I would like this to be put on record, that her reason for keeping silence so far was not to evade her responsibilities, but out of pity for a family of which she has been a member for several years. . . .

'A jury will ultimately have to express its opinion. We are not putting the Lachaumes in the dock here, but she, who knew them better than we do, has succeeded, for a few days at least, in finding extenuating circumstances for them. . . .'

He sat down, in satisfaction, and straightened his tie.

Paulette Lachaume, not knowing where to start from, began by murmuring:

'For a week, since that letter was intercepted, and specially since I'd caught sight of Léonard on the Quai de Bourbon, I'd been afraid . . .'

If this had been the Quai des Orfèvres, Maigret would have spared her a difficult confession, for he would have told the story himself and she would only have had to agree or, where necessary, to correct him.

'Go on, Madame. . . .'

She was not accustomed to talking in front of a stenographer who took down all she said. It intimidated her. She was groping for words, and several times Maigret had a job to keep from interfering. He had forgotten to put out his pipe, and was still smoking it, in his corner, without realizing the fact.

'It was Léonard who frightened me most, for it was he who kept the firm going, at all costs. . . . Once, a long time ago, when I didn't want to give him a sum that was bigger than usual, he made a speech to me, comparing big business firms to old aristocratic families. . . .

' "We have no right," he said, looking very stern, "to let a firm like ours go out of business. . . . I'd do anything on earth rather than let that happen. . . ."

'I remembered that just lately. . . . I almost walked out of the house at once, without a word, to stay at an hotel until the divorce had gone through. . . .'

'What prevented you?'

'I don't know. I wanted to play the game to the end, everything to be done fairly. . . . It's difficult to explain. . . . You'd need to have lived in that house for years, in order to understand. . . . Armand is a weakling, a sick man, the mere shadow of his brother. . . . And I'd grown fond of Jean-Paul. . . . At the beginning I hoped I'd have children. . . . They hoped so too, were always watching for signs of pregnancy. . . . They were terribly disappointed when nothing happened. . . .

'I wonder if that wasn't why Léonard . . .'

She changed the subject.

'It's true Jacques gave me a revolver. . . . I didn't want to take it. . . . I was afraid it would

177

be found. . . . At night I used to put it on my bedside table, and in the daytime I kept it in my handbag. . . .'

'Where is it now?'

'I don't know what *they* did with it. Everything was so confused and so crazy, *after* . . .'

'Tell us what happened *before*.'

'I got in about midnight. . . . Half past eleven, perhaps. . . . I didn't notice the time. . . . I'd decided that in any case this was to be the last night but one . . . . I jumped when I saw Léonard's door opening. . . . He watched me go into my room without a word, without saying good night, and that scared me. . . . On my way to the bathroom, after I'd undressed, I saw light under his door. . . . I was even more frightened. . . . It may have been a presentiment. . . . I felt inclined not to get into bed, to sit in an arm-chair and wait in the dark till daybreak. . . .'

'Did you take your sleeping drug?'

'No. I didn't dare. . . . In the end I lay down, with the gun within reach, determined not to fall asleep. I kept my eyes open, listening to the sounds in the house. . . .'

'You heard him coming?'

'More than an hour went by. . . . I think I dozed off for a moment. . . . Then I heard the boards creak in the corridor. . . . I sat up in bed. . . .'

'Your door was not locked?'

'There's no key; hardly any doors in the house have keys, and the lock had been out of order for ages. . . . I had the impression that someone was turning the handle, and then I crept carefully out of bed and flattened myself against the wall, a yard away.'

'Was there a light in the passage?'

'No. Someone came in. I couldn't see anything. I was afraid to shoot too soon, because I was certain that if I missed . . .'

She could not remain seated any longer. She jumped up and went on, looking now not at the magistrate, but at Maigret:

'I could hear someone's breath coming closer. A body nearly touched me. I'm positive an arm was raised to strike at the place on the bed which my head ought to have been. Then, without realizing it, I pressed the trigger. . . .'

Maigret had suddenly frowned. Suddenly careless of his status, he burst out:

'Will you allow me, *Monsieur le Juge*?'

He continued, without waiting for a reply:

'Who turned on the light?'

'I didn't. . . . At least I don't remember doing so. . . . I rushed out into the corridor, without knowing where I was going. . . . I'd probably have run into the street in my nightdress . . .'

'Who did you run into?'

'My husband . . . I suppose it was he who put the light on. . . .'

'He was fully dressed?'

She looked at him with round eyes. After an effort, as though trying to form a definite picture, she murmured:

'Yes. . . . That hadn't occurred to me. . . .'

'What happened?'

'I must have screamed. . . . Anyhow, I remember opening my mouth to do so. . . . Then I fainted. . . . It wasn't till later that the nightmare began. . . . My father-in-law had come down. . . . So had Catherine. . . . It was her voice one heard most. . . . I could hear her in the distance, ordering Jean-Paul back to his room. . . . I saw Armand coming out of my room with a big spanner. . . .'

'The spanner Léonard had tried to hit you with.'

'I suppose so. . . . They ordered me to be quiet, to stop moaning. . . .'

'Who were *they*?'

'My father-in-law. . . . That old witch Catherine. . . . She most of all! . . . It was she who washed the floor and helped Armand to carry the body. . . . And it was she who noticed that there was blood on my sheet, because Léonard had fallen across the turned-down bed. . . .'

'Did they seem astonished at what had happened?' the examining magistrate now asked.

'I wouldn't say that. . . . Distressed, but not astonished. . . . It seemed to be me they were angry with. . .'

The magistrate resumed:

'It was then that they got busy with the ladder and the windowpane?'

'No.'

Maigret took over again.

'Remember, *Monsieur le Juge*, that about ten o'clock that evening, someone, most probably

180

Léonard, had been seen smashing the broken glass on the wall. . . . At about the same time, no doubt, somebody attended to the ladder, the marks on the window-sill, the window-pane smeared with soap. . .'

She sighed:

'I suppose so. . . .'

Radel began:

'As you see, gentlemen, my client . . .'

'Just a moment!'

The magistrate took a dry, severe tone.

'Who asked you to say nothing and allow the idea of a burglary to be put forward?'

'No one in particular.'

'I'm afraid I don't understand.'

Of course he didn't! He'd been stuffed with theories, and expected the truth to adapt itself to them, to fit into one category or another.

Paulette replied, regardless of putting the magistrate's back up:

'It's easy to see you didn't live through that night! . . . I ended by not knowing what was true and what wasn't. . . . For instance I seem to remember, without being sure it really happened, Catherine's voice croaking:

' "The windows!"

'Because at first they'd turned on all the lights. There are no shutters to the windows, only curtains that don't quite meet in the middle. . . . She had all the lights put out. . . .

'It was she, too, who found an electric torch, in the kitchen, I imagine. . . .

'Then she came back with a bucket. . . .

181

' "You'd do better to get to bed, Monsieur Armand. . . . You too, Monsieur Félix. . . ."'

'But they both stayed there. Another time I asked for some brandy and they wouldn't give it me, saying I mustn't have a drunkard's breath in the morning. . . .'

'What happened in the morning? Did they tell Jean-Paul?'

'No! They told him his uncle had had an attack. . . . When he maintained that he'd heard a shot, everyone assured him it must have been the noise of a train, or a car on the quay, that he'd heard in his sleep. . . .

'As soon as he'd gone off to school, there was a kind of rehearsal. . . .'

She glanced at her lawyer. Was she about to add that she had rung him up to ask his advice? Did he motion to her to keep quiet?

For the last few seconds Maigret had stopped listening, straining his ear. to catch a faint sound, as of something brushing against the door.

Just as Paulette was about to resume her story, there was a sharp report, followed by hurried steps, the murmuring of voices.

In the space of a second, the five people in the magistrate's office had stiffened like wax effigies.

There was a knock on the door. Maigret was the first to get up, slowly, and before he opened the door he said quietly, in Paulette's direction:

'I think your husband is dead.'

Armand was sprawled on the dusty floor. He

had shot himself in the mouth, and within a few inches of his clenched hand lay a 6.35 automatic.

Then Maigret looked back at the motionless young woman, at the lawyer, who had turned slightly pale, at the magistrate, who had not yet had time to strike an attitude.

All he said was:

'I take it you don't need me any more, *Monsieur le Juge*?'

He made no further remark before walking away along the corridor, towards the small door that led into Police Headquarters.

If all this had taken place through there, perhaps it would have gone differently?

Paulette Lachaume had made a regulation confession.

Her husband had died a regulation death.

Who could say whether that might not be the best thing for both of them?

Now only the three old people were left in the home on the Quai de la Gare, and the descendant of the Lachaumes of 1817 was a boarder at school.

The moment Maigret set foot in his office, Lucas sprang out of the next room, with a question on the tip of his tongue. The chief-inspector had already picked up the telephone to ask for Véronique's number, in the Rue François Ier.

It would take her some time to get over things; meanwhile she was certainly entitled to know what had happened.

Noland, 23 October, 1958.